The

Love Child's

REVENGE

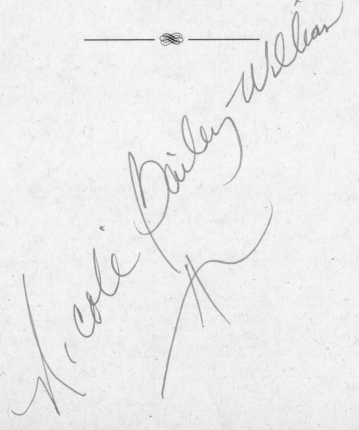

Also by Nicole Bailey-Williams

A Little Piece of Sky

Floating

The

Love Child's

REVENGE

NICOLE BAILEY-WILLIAMS

Broadway Books
New York

Published in the United States by Broadway Books,
an imprint of The Doubleday Publishing Group,
a division of Random House, Inc., New York.
www.broadwaybooks.com

BROADWAY BOOKS and its logo, a letter B bisected on the diagonal, are
trademarks of Random House, Inc.

Library of Congress Cataloging-in-Publication Data

Bailey-Williams, Nicole.
The love child's revenge / by Nicole Bailey-Williams. — 1st ed.
p. cm.
1. Illegitimate children—Fiction. 2. Disinheritance—Fiction.
3. African American women—Fiction. 4. Women television
personalities—Fiction. 5. African Americans—Fiction.
6. Revenge—Fiction. 7. Philadelphia (Pa.)—Fiction.
8. Domestic fiction. I. Title.
PS3552.A3748L68 2008
813'.54—dc22
2008010095

ISBN 978-0-7679-1911-1

PRINTED IN THE UNITED STATES OF AMERICA

1 3 5 7 9 10 8 6 4 2

First Edition

To Underdogs

AND THE LAST SHALL BE FIRST.

Acknowledgments

I need to thank . . .

God for the gift;

my husband for plugging away while I juggled;

my parents for caring for the baby while I wrote, and for everything else that they do;

my editors, Janet Hill and Christian Nwachukwu, Jr., for their faith in my work;

my agent, Elaine Koster;

my fellow scribes Marita Golden, Patricia Haley, Victoria Christopher Murray, Kenji Jasper, Mat Johnson, and Ravi Howard for making this profession a little less solitary; Sampson Davis, MD, for contributing medical information; and E. Lynn Harris for embracing and teaching my books at the University of Arkansas;

my Delta Sorors, specifically the Quaker City Alumnae Chapter and Dana Davis Moore of Chesterfield Alumnae;

my publicists, Vanessa Lloyd-Sgamabti and Laura Pillar;

my librarian supporters, Sara Goddard MacAteer, Andy Kahan, Drew Birden, and Sandy Farrell, for always putting together great events for me;

my former student Carla Glosson for typing for me; and

my readers for their e-mails and continued loyalty.

The

Love Child's

REVENGE

Prologue

It had taken me weeks to read all of the letters that had been locked in my mother's bedroom, the bedroom that I couldn't bear to enter after she died in my junior year of college. But the summer after graduation, before I left for my new job in Atlanta, I dove in, searching for the letter that my father had written around the time of my conception. It was dated February 16, and in ink that had purpled with time on the cream linen paper, his words leapt from the page.

Dear Georgia,
You're right. You're absolutely right. A child is a reminder of why we're alive, and giving birth is a way to assist God in a miracle. But you've got to know that you . . . this . . . caught me off guard. I'm not angry,

*though. Just shocked. And since we've always been honest
with each other, I have to admit that I'm a bit pleased. Not
at the circumstances, you see, because that shames me. I
shouldn't be in such a predicament with my situation, but
I can't think of a better person to help shape a life for me
than you.*

*I know that most would think me a fool for even writing
about this, but that only shows you my trust in you. I
know that you'll always do the right thing, and I want you
to know that I'll always do the right thing by you and the
little one. That I promise you.*

*In closing, my sweet, I want to thank you for the
opportunity that you've given me. Maybe this child will
respect and love me in a way that, despite my best efforts,
the others don't.*

Loving you,
LH

So that was it. He had been happy about me from the
beginning. Although I still was what they, his legitimate
family, had called me, a bastard, I found validation in the
knowledge that I had been created in love and that he, my
father, Louis Harrison, loved me even as I grew in Momma's
belly.

My Dear Georgia,

*As your belly begins to round, you can't know how
beautiful you look. Your face holds a glow that makes you
look even more angelic. Even though you are in a difficult
situation, you remain steady and the sweetest person I
know. That makes me treasure you even more. Thank you*

for being who you are, and thank you for loving me and
taking such good care of me.

Yours,

LH

My father believed in owning property. From the first lot that he purchased, on which he built his lucrative funeral parlor, he learned that if a man had nothing else, he needed a place to hang his hat. Over time, he amended that sentiment, stating, "It's a poor rat that has only one hole to run into." So he bought properties right and left, acquiring them through sheriff sales and auctions, and set them aside for his children, shoring up their financial footing. A birthday present here, a graduation gift there, a sweet-sixteen souvenir here, a Valentine's present there—in all, he was rumored to have owned more than one hundred properties throughout the city. My first property was a Christmas present.

Georgia,

I told you that I'd do right by our beautiful baby girl.
I'll do right by you, too. You're in my will, so if I should
pass before you, contact my attorney. I just wanted you to
know that last week I bought a multi-unit row house in
Kensington for her. I'll get a copy of the deed to you soon.

Love you both,

LH

Every time he made a purchase, he sent a brief note, giving the address and reiterating his promise to do right by me. A duplex in The Tinderlines, a storefront in East Falls, a multi-unit in Port Richmond . . . the list went on and on.

Twenty-five properties in all. On paper, I was a very rich woman. I found the name of his attorney in one of his notes, and I called his office, anxiously waiting to hear what I needed to do to claim the property.

"Randolph and Sofansky," the receptionist said.

"Hello. My name is Claudia Fryar, and I'd like to speak with Justin Randolph."

"Mr. Randolph is in a meeting right now. May I ask the nature of your call?"

"Yes, it's regarding some property left to me by Louis Harrison."

"Oh, yes, Mr. Harrison. I'll make a note of your call and give the message to Mr. Randolph. Where can Mr. Randolph reach you?"

I gave her the number, and I sat down at the table, pondering the value of my property. I was angry that I hadn't known about it before. If I had, I'd have been able to finish my education with my dignity in check, never having compromised myself with John Freeman. But that was water under the bridge. I'd still proceed according to plan, working my way north and getting experience in my field; but with the confidence that money could bring, I'd never have to do anything I didn't want to.

The phone rang sooner than I expected it to, and Justin Randolph was on the other end.

"Ms. Fryar?"

"Mr. Randolph. Thanks for getting back to me so quickly."

"Certainly."

"I'll speak bluntly, Mr. Randolph. Louis Harrison was my father. I just found out recently, although I've known him my whole life. He was my mother's employer, so I actually grew up with him, but I didn't know about the paternity."

4

"I see," he replied noncommittally.

"It recently came to my attention that he purchased some property for me, and I'd like to see what I need to do to claim it."

"Ms. Fryar, is it possible for you to come to our Philadelphia office?" he asked in a tone that worried me. Although it was difficult to tell with attorneys, if it had been good news, he would have sounded more optimistic.

"Well, yes, but it would take a little time. Is there something wrong, Mr. Randolph?"

"Why don't we discuss it when you get here?"

"Okay," I said hesitantly.

"Good. I'll transfer you to my secretary. She'll put you on my schedule at a time most convenient for you."

"Okay. Thank you, Mr. Randolph."

"See you soon," he said, hanging up.

I scheduled a meeting for just after I got to Atlanta, where I was beginning my career in television, giving myself enough time to get unpacked before flying off to Philly to find out about my future. I shouldn't have been so hopeful.

When I arrived in Philadelphia two weeks later, I found myself sitting across from Justin Randolph, who could have passed for white, what with his freckled skin, green eyes, and graying hair that fell in loose waves. Yet the Morehouse College degree on his wall and fraternity mug on his desk removed any traces of doubt about his racial identity.

"Ms. Fryar, Louis Harrison was a generous man, and I respected him greatly," he offered.

"Yes, he was," I replied, anxious to hear the reason why he had dragged me all the way up here from Georgia.

"I've asked someone else to join us, and he should be arriving momentarily."

"Okay. You sounded a little vague when I spoke with you. Is there any reason that I should be alarmed?"

"I'll let Mr. Elkins answer that when he gets here."

"And who is he?" I asked, trying to maintain my composure despite the fact that I was growing more and more nervous with each passing minute.

"His company manages the Harrison properties."

The door opened just then, and in walked Meridius Elkins, a middle-aged man whose coloring reminded me of one of the Philadelphia soft pretzels I'd been craving ever since I left the city all those years ago. In fact, my first order of business once I'd landed at Philly International had been to buy one from an airport vendor.

"Meridius," Mr. Randolph said, rising to shake his hand.

"Justin," he replied before turning to look at me.

"This is Claudia Fryar, Louis Harrison's other daughter," Justin Randolph said, introducing me with a nod.

I didn't like the way Randolph said "other," but I knew that he did it to distinguish me from Elizabeth and Louise Harrison, whom he'd undoubtedly met at some point.

"Nice to meet you," I said, taking Elkins's hand.

"My pleasure."

"Meridius, Ms. Fryar called me a few weeks ago to inquire about the properties that her father bought for her."

"Yes," I asserted, speaking up for myself. "In his letters to my mother, he wrote that he'd purchased twenty-five properties for me. I have addresses for most of them."

I handed the letters to Mr. Elkins, who briefly looked them over before handing them to Mr. Randolph.

"May I have my secretary copy these?"

I nodded my approval, and he walked to the door, popping his head and hand out and speaking quietly to his secretary.

"I'm glad that you have these letters. They might help you, depending on how you plan to proceed," Justin Randolph said. "At least, you can put a stop to all of this."

"Stop to all of what?" I asked.

Meridius Elkins cleared his throat before speaking: "I'm not sure exactly why he did it, though I assume it was in order to avoid embarrassing his wife, but the properties that Louis Harrison bought for you were put in his name in trust for you. You were to inherit them when you turned twenty-one. When he died five years ago, I spoke to his wife about all of the property, and with regard to that block of property—"

"My property, you mean."

"Yes," he said, a little exasperated, "your property. She instructed me to cease paying taxes on that property, and little by little the houses have gone up for auction through the sheriff's office for tax delinquencies."

"What are you saying?" I asked, feeling my body heat rise up my neck, warming my face. "Do I have anything left?"

"You do. Just not what you had."

"So from twenty-five properties, I'm down to . . ." I paused to let him finish the sentence for me.

"Eleven."

"Eleven," I shrieked. "That's less than half."

"But it's more than you knew you had just one month ago," Justin Randolph interjected.

I cut my eyes at him. "So I should just be happy with what I've got, then, right?"

"It sounds rather heartless, Ms. Fryar, but I'd say yes."

"I have a question. Why didn't anyone contact me about my inheritance?"

"Apparently, there was no forwarding address for you and your mother, and according to Mrs. Harrison, her private detective was unable to locate you."

"You mean the same woman who instructed you to stop paying taxes on my property is the same woman whose word you took about not being able to locate me?" I asked, incredulous.

The room was silent as I considered my options. Either pay the back taxes on the remaining properties, collect the accumulated rents that were rightfully mine, and call it a day, or begin a lawsuit against Eliza Harrison and sue the city to get back my properties, some of which may have already been sold.

"What's your pleasure, Ms. Fryar?" Justin Randolph questioned.

"Of course, you don't think that I can answer that question on the spot," I snapped.

"Of course not, but remember that time is of the essence. Just about every month, at least one of your properties is coming up for sheriff sale."

Meridius Elkins handed me a thick file filled with spreadsheets containing notations about all of my father's properties: their locations, their appraised values, their upkeep expenses, and the incomes they'd brought in over time. The remaining properties still made me a very comfortable woman, just not as rich as I'd been on paper.

"Gentlemen," I said, standing. "I'll get back to you soon."

They stood as well.

Mr. Randolph offered, "I'll be in the office until seven this evening. Please call if you'd like to talk."

"Certainly. Thank you, Mr. Elkins, Mr. Randolph," I said, shaking their hands. "I'll be in touch."

I walked out of the Center City office and back to my hotel, where I sat at a table in the bar, examining the file more closely. Truly, I don't know why I was surprised, but I couldn't believe that Eliza Harrison would stoop so low as to steal my inheritance. I'd done nothing to her—besides serve as a reminder of her husband's infidelity. But that wasn't my fault. Children have no control over the circumstances of their birth, so why would she do that to me?

1

As I surveyed the crowded room where the Women to Watch luncheon was being held, I felt a surge of pride, thinking, "I am a phoenix, rising from the ashes and re-creating myself from dust. Where decay once dominated, opportunity abounds. Where poverty once prevailed, abundance now reigns. Where shame once ruled, pride now resides. And I stand among them unbowed, uncowed, with my head held high. It's been a long time coming, and there are things that I certainly would have done differently if circumstances had been different. But they weren't. Like Old Blue Eyes, I did it my way, and now I sit at the table among those who once thought me worthless, and *I* am The Grande Dame."

Since graduating from Moultrie State University, it had taken me seven years to get back to the City of Brotherly

Love. After seven years of toil, now, as at jubilee, I was finally enjoying the fruits of my labor. I had to admit that I did have some fun along the way, and I definitely learned a lot and built up my arsenal. And as I made progress, I realized that I was retracing Momma's steps north, where she had headed roughly a quarter of a century before, chasing a dream that she never caught. But now I'd caught it, wrapped it up, and presented it to myself with a big, luscious bow on top.

Finally I was the television personality and news anchor that I'd always wanted to be. I had lots of fans, and people loved me. They waited on my word. To them I was important, not someone to be overlooked as I had been in the past. As I made my way on this path, I wasn't concerned about market size or making continuous moves from smaller markets to progressively larger ones. My only aim was to follow my mother's footsteps and return north, where I could show the Philadelphia elite that I, too, was worthy. Hell, I was more than worthy. And they'd better not forget it.

My first stop after leaving Moultrie, Georgia, was Atlanta, where I was a traffic reporter. It was a great place to cut my teeth, and my job helped me learn my way around affluent communities like Lenox Hill and others I dreamed of living in. I explored them all on my downtime, admiring the grand homes that would cost three times as much in northern cities. Every night after my "dream drives," I'd return to my apartment and practice speaking in front of the mirror and work on my carriage and poise with the aim of developing a presence for the camera as well as perfecting my on-air delivery. Despite being pleased that I was starting in the city that folks were calling "the new black mecca," I knew that dissatisfaction and eventual boredom wouldn't allow me to stay in the same job for very long. Besides, I was eager to get back home to Philadelphia to claim my rightful place in society. Nine months later, I burst forth from the Peach State, heading to the next location on my trek north.

Residents of Columbia, South Carolina, welcomed me as a new weather reporter for the FBC affiliate. This was before the push for weather people to become certified meteorologists, so a vampish vixen of a weather girl would do. I pushed the envelope a bit, though, wearing revealing clothes while reporting on steamy summer days, or sporting a bikini under a fur—long before Naked News but long enough after one of my journalism idols had done the same that people had forgotten. At other times I was all smiles, forecasting everything from sun to storms. I got the attention of the viewers and of the general manager, who began lingering around the set when I was on. Coy and coquettish, I smiled pleasantly as he attempted to endear himself to me. When he put his arm around my shoulders one day as I was exiting the crowded set, that was all the ammunition I needed to cry sexual harassment. Enough people had seen him regularly fawning over me that contacting an attorney was merely a formality. So after about two years I left the station with a five-figure settlement and a stellar recommendation letter. Next stop Durham, North Carolina.

In Durham I got my first real break, reporting the early and midday news. Even though the job gave me the opportunity to be on camera with regularity, I called my duty "shit detail" because I was stationed in one of the suburban bureaus where not much news took place. The occasional early morning fire, the rare small-town political scandal—you name it, I covered it. The producers knew that I was willing to work hard, so when they needed me to step in for an absent evening reporter, I jumped in with both feet. That opportunity presented itself frequently enough that I felt confident in officially applying for the spot when the regular reporter left for another city. I figured, why shouldn't I apply? I spoke well, I was quick on my feet, and I had the experience. Unfortunately, I was beaten out by a Barbie look-alike from the Dallas station. Then a consumer reporter's position became available, and I put in my bid for that as well. After observing the way the station was run, I wasn't surprised when the spot went to a Jackie O clone with an underbite. Tired of bumping my head against the glass ceiling, after little more than a year I knew that it was time to leave Durham, so I headed north to Richmond, Virginia.

Although it wasn't really what I wanted, I landed an arts and entertainment job at the FBC affiliate there. I had been trying to establish myself as a serious journalist who was spunky enough to compete with Katie Couric, intelligent enough to knock Katharine Graham on her ass, and compassionate enough to give Oprah a run for her money, so this job seemed like a step backward. It wasn't without its perks, though. I received passes to all kinds of cultural events, and I got to meet artists, authors, dancers, and musicians. And Richmond was the place where my fame in the community blossomed. I was asked to give presentations at a variety of events, and I did my fair share of the prestigious ones with good perks while turning down the low-profile events. Then I was asked to emcee an event sponsored by the Richmond Alumnae Chapter of Delta Alpha Zeta.

The sorority had been courting me since I'd arrived in Richmond, inviting me to their events and even honoring me with an award. I was pleasantly surprised when they sent me an invitation for membership, and knowing about the privileges that membership brought, I accepted and was initiated in a special weekend ceremony.

So there I stood, the newest member of the chapter, and I was more than a little nervous as I listened to the chapter president introduce me. As she read my credentials to the crowd who had come for the art auction, I almost forgot that she was talking about me. I had augmented some of my accomplishments, making myself look more like a humanitarian than I was. Service projects I had supposedly initiated and charitable contributions I had purportedly made painted me in the image of a modern-day Mother Teresa. Only I was much sexier.

". . . And so it is with great pleasure and profound pride that I introduce our emcee for the evening, our soror, Peach Harrison," she announced, beaming.

A few of the younger sorors gave the Delta Alpha Zeta call as the older ones applauded. I heard a few of the men whistle as I marched to the podium wrapped in an air of false confidence. Despite the fact that I made my living by talking, doing it with a live, visible audience sometimes made my stomach flip, especially afterward, when I would rush to the ladies' room and heave until my stomach was empty.

"Good evening, beautiful people of Richmond, Virginia," I said, smiling. I was poise and polish personified, never letting on that I was quaking inside. This greeting, which I used when I reported on arts and culture events, initiated a hearty round of applause. "I'm Peach Harrison, and I am honored to greet you on behalf of my dazzling, dynamic sorors of Delta Alpha Zeta Sorority, Incorporated. Welcome to the Sixth Annual Art Auction. You will be glad to know that last year the beautiful people in the Richmond area raised $223,000 for the service projects the sorority sponsors. This year we are going to raise even more, because we know the women of this chapter and we know their hearts. Our sorors are making a difference, and tonight, with your contributions, you will, too."

I had surveyed the crowded room, noting that the ladies were dripping with expensive jewelry. Lagos, David Yurman, and Mikimoto twinkled from their delicate wrists, ears, fingers, and throats. The men oozed opulence in dark jackets and brightly colored pants that only the rich or the drunk are confident or oblivious enough to wear.

Some of the artists were in attendance to autograph their works and to give insight about their creations. In the days before the auction I had scanned the catalogue, seeing familiar names of artists living and dead whose original works would be auctioned tonight. William H. Johnson, Jacob Lawrence, and Romare Bearden were among them. So was Ron "Boriqua Soul" Juarez, the sexy middleweight boxing champ who painted canvases by day and pounded opponents by night.

"Before we get to the auction, I have some special guests that I'd like to acknowledge."

When I called the names of the artists in attendance, I noticed that Juarez stared at me extra long, grinning broadly. I nodded in acknowledgment and continued, nonplussed.

Since leaving Moultrie, I hadn't been in a relationship with anyone. I had been so busy working and plotting my next move that I hadn't made time. Truthfully, I hadn't really been interested in anyone. Besides Ishmael, with whom I'd been obsessed since our days at Moultrie State. And I was leap years away from roping him. But if there really was a lid for every pot, as Momma used to say, then he was my Calphalon lid, and I longed for him to find his way to me, his pot. But for now it looked as if Juarez was trying to clutter up the meantime while I waited for Ishmael.

While the other artists stood and waved where they were, he made his way to me at the podium, carrying a glass of white wine. He raised an eyebrow before puckering up and blowing me a kiss. I smiled at his gesture, amused yet a little annoyed because he'd almost broken my composure. I couldn't help but notice, however, that despite the ferocity of his sport, his face was virtually scar free.

Bidding was fierce, especially on the Bearden pieces. Throughout the evening, Juarez made very public, almost embarrassing overtures to me. When the time came for me to auction off two of his originals, he surprised me by asking to take the mic.

"¡Hola! I'm glad that the members of the sorority invited me to be here. The pieces that I donated for the evening are very special, because they were done during the time that I was training for the title, which you know I won."

A round of applause went up from the boxing fans in the audience.

"But there is one thing that I need your help with this evening. I won't sign any of my work unless our emcee here agrees to have dinner with me tomorrow."

All eyes turned to me, and audience members gasped and giggled in humorous expectation. Juarez began a chant: "Peach! Peach! Peach!"

The room seemed to shrink as I looked around. Lord knows that I liked the attention, but I didn't need Mr. Ron

"Boriqua Soul" Juarez to throw me off my course. Judging from the sound of the crowd, though, I didn't have much choice but to acquiesce to his advances.

"Okay. But I get to pick the restaurant," I said, trying to regain control of the situation.

"That's fine by me," he said, smiling. As he kissed my hand the crowd cheered, and I spent the rest of the evening allowing him to fawn over me.

Even though I had made the dinner reservations for us at an upscale Spanish restaurant, Juarez dominated the date. First he insisted that we sit at a table by the window. Then he ordered for me without asking me what I wanted to eat. After dinner he took my hand and led me to the dance floor, where he guided me through salsa and mambo numbers. One thing that I love about Latin dancing is the opportunity it gives you to slide into cruise control while the man takes the lead. As ironic as it sounds, it's satisfying for me to surrender to a man, because I've never had anyone to shoulder my burdens with or for me. But while I admire decisiveness in a man, I also appreciate being consulted, which was something he didn't seem to get. Rather than complain, I just sucked it up and rode it for what it was worth.

Apparently, the evening was worth a whole lot more than I thought it was. A quick look at *The Richmond Tattler*'s gossip column on Monday confirmed it. Not only was there a paragraph about us leading the column, but there were two photographs as well, one from Saturday's auction and one from Sunday's date as we sat by the window of the restaurant. I knew that sorors had contacted Richmond's media outlets to cover Saturday's event, but I'm sure they would have preferred that the attention be focused on them and their community service rather than my love life. At least they got a mention, though. Without needing confirmation, I knew that Juarez was responsible for Sunday's photo. I vacillated between the annoyance I felt at being manipulated by him and the vulnerability I felt at being violated by the photographer.

For the sake of closure, I called Juarez on Monday night to hear his reaction. As I suspected he would, he tried to minimize the issue, saying, "Come on, *bonita*. Don't be angry. At least the photographer caught your good side."

"That's hardly the point," I retorted, suddenly eager to get off the phone.

"You're right. *Lo siento*. I apologize. I don't mean to make light of your feelings. I'm just gearing up for my next fight, when I have to defend my title. It's two months away, and my manager advised me to take the opposite approach from my opponent."

My annoyance was being replaced by intrigue. "What approach is that?" I asked despite myself.

"Killer Calderón is playing crazy. Leaking information that he trains by scrapping with his pit bulls for raw meat and crazy shit like that. My manager has this idea that I should make it look like training is the last thing on my mind. That will make him super confident. In the meantime, I'll spend my days training like mad."

"I see," I said, my annoyance returning. "So I'm the showpiece that solidifies your 'don't care' attitude, huh?"

"It's not like that, *bonita*."

"That's sure how it sounds."

"Trust me. You are too fine a woman for me to just leave hangin'."

"Flattery gets you nowhere with me. I already know that I'm fine."

"*¿Verdad?* Do you now?"

"Absolutely."

"Confidence in a woman is truly appealing."

"I'm glad you think so. And by the by, I've got a mind. Don't take liberties with me like you did last night."

"What do you mean?"

"Like ordering for me."

"*Lo siento, bonita.* I didn't realize I was offending you: Cultural difference."

"From what I've heard, you're only half Latino. Thus the Boriqua *Soul*."

"Touché."

"It doesn't matter. Anyway, just don't let it happen again."

"Damn, you're tough. Tougher than Killer Calderón."

"And don't you forget it."

The next few weeks were a whirlwind of activities, and though I hated to admit it, "Boriqua Soul" was growing on me. A little. Despite his pushy insistence, I demanded that I stay in alone a couple of nights a week, and when we did go out, I always retired to my place. We did have fun, though, and being seen with him was doing wonders for my popularity both in the city and at the station. The urgent e-mail that I got from my general manager was confirmation that people were talking.

"Peach, I've got something to ask you about Juarez," Colt Blackson said to me after I was settled into a seat across the desk from him.

"Let's hear it, Colt."

"You know, of course, that the Juarez-Calderón fight is about a month away."

I waited for him to tell me something I didn't know. The station was constantly abuzz with news of my escapades with Juarez. Skydiving together into Capitol Square during evening rush hour. Paying big money to restaurateurs to cancel long-standing reservations and rent out their establishments to us for the evening. Cruising up the James River in a gondola. As a couple, we were the hottest thing to hit Richmond in a long time. So as I looked at Colt I simply blinked to get him to continue.

"We've been trying to get a one-on-one exclusive with him for weeks, but the only thing we've been able to get is the press conference that he held for all of the networks at a downtown hotel. You obviously have an in, so I'm hoping that you'll use it."

"What's in it for me?" I asked. I wasn't stupid enough to lay the foundation for Jack Reese, the arrogant sportscaster, to step on top of, locking myself out in the cold. Colt reddened, and by the way he cleared his throat, I could tell that's exactly what he'd been thinking.

"A wonderful opportunity. You'll have a ten-minute slot with him on *Sports Extra* on the night of the fight."

The opportunity sounded delicious, but I remained stoic, unwilling to look too eager. "Let me think it over, and I'll get back to you in the morning."

Colt's jaw dropped slightly, and I could tell that he was shocked by my boldness. But he quickly recovered, clearing his throat again.

"Okay, I'll look to hear from you by eleven," he said, trying to reassert his authority.

I walked out of his office poised and confident. This assignment would demonstrate my versatility, proving that I could wear many hats. From traffic reporter to weather reporter, news reporter to arts and entertainment reporter, I had definitely been working my way up the ranks. This new challenge as a sports reporter was just that. A challenge. There weren't many women in that arena, but I already knew that I had it in me. Colt Blackson was making me prove myself and earn my stripes in the same way that I'd had to do all of my life. From the tormentors of my youth to a variety of nameless, faceless news producers in all of the cities where I had worked, they were all the same. They thought so little of me, but I'd shown them. This interview with Juarez was going to be the best one they'd ever seen. He'd give me access to his world that other reporters would never get.

I checked my clock when I returned to my office. One-thirty. Juarez would be on a break from his rigorous training schedule.

"¡Hola, bonita!"

"I'm not going to keep you, but I need a favor."

"Anything for you."

"Don't be so quick to say that. You don't know what it is."

"Whatever it is you want, I'm willing," he said provocatively. We'd done nothing more than kiss, but it wasn't because he hadn't tried.

"I don't want it to appear that I'm using our relationship to better my career, because that's not my style. I wouldn't do that," I lied easily.

"I know."

"But my GM asked me about the possibility of getting an exclusive before the fight."

"Sure," he said without a thought.

"Don't you need to confer with someone? Your manager or someone?"

"I'm a man, baby. I make decisions for myself."

"I know, but I just thought that—"

Juarez interrupted: "Any way that I can help you."

It was one of those rare moments of sweetness I saw in people that made me wish I were a different kind of person. It made me wish that I could be unconditionally kind. But I wasn't, for little unconditional kindness had been shown to me. Everything I had gotten I'd worked for, on my hands and knees or on my back, and with Juarez I knew that I'd have to pay the piper at some point.

We shot hours of footage of him training, conferring with his manager, sparring with his partner, and painting in the studio in his house. Then I donned a tank top and some white satin boxing shorts with a black waistband and a stripe down the side, contrasting with his white-trimmed black ones, and we stepped inside the ring at the gym. We made a show of our playful sparring and some fake body shots and uppercuts I threw at his chin. Then we pulled some chairs into the center of the ring, where I asked him some tough questions. The result was an edgy, gritty, almost sexy piece that Colt loved, gushing over it in his meeting with the producers. The fact that Juarez won made Colt even happier, because he had bet on the bout. The spot was so successful that I incorporated it into my audition tape, knowing that I could parlay it into a bigger gig at the next stop on my northbound odyssey. Eventually I hoped to do a national show, but this interview would go a long way in demonstrating my versatility.

The interview was almost foreplay for the fierce fight, which was attended by just under five thousand. Local and national politicians, members of Richmond's business community, local celebrities, and fight lovers garbed themselves in everything from animal skins to fine silks as they crowded into the arena to see what was dubbed "The Fight of the Decade." I wasn't especially passionate about pugilism, but I sat ringside and shouted my support for Boriqua Soul anyway.

"*Bonita*, you'll distract me, sitting so close during the fight," he'd said as I drove him to the arena on the night of the fight.

"I definitely don't want to do that," I'd responded. "Just think of it this way as you make your way around the ring: After tonight's fight, I'll let you rest so that you can rejuvenate yourself. You'll need every ounce of strength you can get in order to tangle with me tomorrow night."

He'd smiled and licked his lips before getting out of the car, and I'd winked and opened the top button of my blouse suggestively before saying, "See you tomorrow at your place."

He danced around the ring with the grace of a gazelle, never acknowledging my presence. He dove in ferociously, attacking Killer Calderón like a lion assailing an antelope, and just as quickly, he retreated. Killer Calderón never seemed to know where Boriqua Soul was coming from until he saw the red gloves centimeters from his face. Headshots and body blows abounded as Boriqua Soul pummeled him, leaving him dumbfounded. Finally, in round five, Killer Calderón just sat down, and the ref began the count.

The night after the fight, I gave Juarez what he had been craving, and he was a happy man. He spoke Spanish in my ear as we twirled in his sheets in frenzied passion, and in the morning I tiptoed out of the house, leaving him nothing but my scent on his sheets.

We didn't see each other after that night. There was no need. We were adults, and we'd known that we were both opportunists who were looking for ways to up the ante. We'd gotten what we wanted, and now I was looking to move on to a different city. He'd been good to me, though, so before I left Richmond for Washington, D.C., I sent him a basket of delectable white peaches and a bucket of sweet cream.

D.C. was the place where I kicked up my career in a big way, with a job as the morning and midday news anchor. I was all smiles as I greeted residents of America's capital and bantered jovially with my cohost, a handsome Hampton alum named Randall Myles. D.C. was also the place where I upped my societal worth by immersing myself in the social scene and becoming an active member of the prestigious Capital City Alumnae Chapter of Delta Alpha Zeta, among other organizations.

"Sorors, this soror doesn't need an introduction. You see her every morning on KDC-Channel 5. She just paid her dues for this year, so let's welcome Soror Peach Harrison to Capital City Alumnae."

The members applauded and smiled warmly at me as I stood at the front of the room with three other new chapter members.

"Thank you, sorors. I just moved to the area, and the first thing I did was look up this chapter, because I love my sorors," I schmoozed, beaming with a million-watt smile. "Just bear with me if I'm a little rusty when we sing our beautiful hymn."

"That's alright," an older soror said, letting me off the hook.

They were thrilled to welcome yet another high-profile

member, so they nodded their approval before welcoming me and turning their attention to the remaining new members.

As I suspected, the membership turned out to be worth every penny of the five hundred dollars in annual dues I paid. Even on college campuses the initiation fee was stiff, higher than at other sororities. By setting high fees, the sorority was able to weed out people who wouldn't be able to financially support its programs. For that reason it was the smallest of the black, Greek-letter sororities, and for that reason the Deltas earned the title of elitists. The members of the Capital City Alumnae Chapter were connected in ways that I had only imagined. Country club memberships, summer homes, boats—these women possessed everything I wanted to possess. Therefore, I was positively thrilled when one of the older sorors took a liking to me and took me under her wing.

Soror Emma Prescott Daley was more refined than Eliza, my mother's former employer in Philadelphia, could ever hope to be. Emma had been married to one of D.C.'s most prominent dentists, who had also owned a horse farm stocked with purebreds that went on to win countless racing titles. In addition to being wealthy, she was by far the most kind and charitable woman I'd ever met, once her veneer was penetrated. In fact, besides myself, she was the only chapter member who donated scholarships in her name to local high school students. She loved that we had that in common, and she liked that I mentored area teenagers who were interested in careers in journalism. She said that she'd like to volunteer with me in mentoring the girls, conducting workshops on etiquette and other social graces. At seventy-three, she was still spry and spirited, and she'd do wonderfully working with young people. Inside the sorority, her support or the lack of it could make or break a proposal. Many new ideas, which tended to unnerve old-guard sorors because of their novelty, passed because Emma spoke in favor of them, swaying the voting membership to her side. Likewise, ideas that had outlived their usefulness were tabled because she spoke against them. People respected her because she was fair and wise. And she had pledged under the sorority's founders. So when she gave me her stamp of approval, I was in like Flynn.

We met for a late lunch once a week, and it was at one of these lunches that she told me why she was so drawn to me.

"You remind me of my granddaughter Wendy," she said. "She was free-spirited and adventurous. Beautiful and sharp as a tack, just like you. She'd be about your age if she were alive."

"What happened to her?" I asked, reaching across the table to touch Emma's hand.

"She died in an accident overseas."

"I'm sorry to hear that, Soror Daley."

"I've told you a dozen times. Call me Emma, or I'll be insulted."

"Yes, ma'am. Emma, I mean."

"Anyway, when I look at you, I see all that Wendy could have become. Like you, she was well-bred. She had the world at her doorstep, but she didn't want the life that we had mapped out for her. She said that teas and cotillions were outdated and elitist." As she spoke Emma stared over my shoulder, her eyes shadowed with the glaze of remembering.

I couldn't imagine anyone not wanting the fortunate life

that an heir of Emma Prescott Daley's would have. The right connections. Few struggles. Opportunity. Financial comfort. It was what I had wanted my whole life. It was what my mother had worked her fingers to the bone to provide. And Wendy had just walked away from it.

"She joined the Peace Corps when she was twenty, and she went to Ghana," Emma continued. "When her time was up, she decided to stay on the continent, and she traveled to South Africa. As an American, she was given 'white status,' but she was cautioned to tread carefully. Hardheaded, strong-willed, call it what you want, that's what she was. She began working with some anti-apartheid activists, and you can imagine the rest. She was arrested and detained, and she was found dead on the side of the road just hours after she was released from police custody. That beautiful, stupid girl. Her life here was made. All she had to do was step into the shoes. Instead, she had to go looking for trouble halfway around the world."

I was saddened by her story. Emma was too nice a person to experience the sadness that kind of tragedy brought. I was surprised by my empathy because I'd grown self-centered over time. But Emma touched something in me, and she made me feel almost human.

Besides sorority life, my involvement with the D.C. chapter of the National Association of Black Journalists, and my friendship with Emma, I had something else to keep me occupied. Randall, my morning and midday news cohost. No, I hadn't softened and given in to what I considered the myth of romance. Overall, I still felt that love was for suckers and men were a distraction I couldn't truly afford. With the exception of Ishmael Taylor, who, unbeknownst to him, held a place in my heart. Juarez had shown me how gossip about romance, feigned or otherwise, could work to my benefit, giving me publicity and my career a boost. So Randall and I promenaded around the city, attending a variety of high-profile events, and I lapped up every minute of the attention, knowing that invitations for paid emcee gigs would come. We never had to pay at restaurants. We always had VIP perks at the clubs we visited. We were the "it" couple, and people actually followed our pseudo romance. From the gaga eyes I openly made at him on air to his hand intentionally lingering long near mine when we came back from a commercial break, viewers were tuning in like mad. It was incredible.

My producer, Siobhan Kimpton, tried to explain the phenomenon as she stood in the doorway of the room where our makeup was being applied: "You're the sweethearts of the morning airwaves. You make people feel optimistic when they wake up, and they face their days feeling good."

"Whatever," I said. "It works."

"You're telling me," she gushed. "Ratings are up, and you two just got invited to host the bridal expo at the convention center on Valentine's weekend."

"What do you say?" I said, turning to Randall, who was sitting in the chair next to mine.

"I'm not sure."

"What?"

"I'll have to see," he said, removing the protective cover from the neckline of his crisply starched shirt after the makeup artist finished with him and exited the room.

"Well, it has to be both of you, or it's a no go," Siobhan said, looking at her clipboard. "Work on him, Peach."

"I sure will," I said, smiling broadly at Siobhan as she left.

I turned my attention to Randall, and my fake smile disappeared. "What do you mean, you're not sure?" I snapped. "You don't get any choices here, sweetness. People love a good old-fashioned romance like our pseudo relationship, and I'm the one who makes the decisions for D.C.'s darling couple."

He looked at me with pure venom in his eyes before gathering his news notes. "You can't keep a hold on me forever," he hissed before storming out of the room to the set.

Checking my reflection in the mirror, I smiled coolly before standing. He'd do whatever I said unless he wanted his secret to get out. The D.C. media circuit was far too conservative to accept the truth about him. In fact, if it got out, it would end his career in Chocolate City. So I knew that I'd get my way, as I always did.

After work, I went shopping at Crystal City Mall in Arlington, Virginia, before heading back to D.C. for an early dinner at Fasika's Ethiopian Restaurant. As I picked at my shrimp tibs with my injera bread, I looked out the window at the people who colored the streets of Adams Morgan, the artsy, eclectic neighborhood not far from Howard University's campus. The handsome assistant manager of the restaurant interrupted my people-watching with his deep, lilting voice.

"Is everything to your liking, Ms. Harrison?"

"As usual, it's delicious," I responded, looking into his eyes. There was something about Ethiopians' eyes that made me melt.

"I'm glad. Thank you for the mention on the show last week. Enjoy your meal with my compliments."

"That's very generous of you," I said, batting my eyes.

"You've proven yourself to be a friend to this restaurant. I thank you," he said, bowing slightly before descending the stairs.

What a charming man, I mused before returning to my meal. Looking out the window again, I spotted a familiar face: Timothy Sanders.

He was handsome, fit, and successful, and he would make some woman a wonderful catch—if he weren't already spoken for. His romantic life was one of D.C.'s best-kept secrets. I had stumbled upon it by accident, and before leaving D.C., where I'd spent twenty-six months, I had milked it for all it was worth.

2

Growing up a seamstress' daughter, I've always had a thing for fabrics, how they can suit a person's personality. I looked over the Dana Buchman steel gray crepe de chine dress I'd worn tonight. Crepe de chine had been one of Momma's favorite fabrics to work with, and I saw why. It was light enough to be crafted into evening wear with ease, yet it didn't have to be formal. It was one of the fabrics that I felt suited my personality best, so I loved buying pieces made from it. With the phone perched on my shoulder, I was hanging up the dress when Miss Mamie's voice piped up on the other end.

"So who was there?" she inquired girlishly as we chatted on the phone later that night. She was in Georgia, where she had lived for twelve years since she sold her thriving soul food restaurant in South Philly. Momma and I had moved there together.

Miss Mamie had been my mother's best friend, and I spoke with her often, trying to fill the gap that had been left by my mother's absence. Tonight I had been telling her about a film festival I'd emceed, torturing her by talking about the décor and food first when I knew she was more interested in who had shown up for the event. The movie that had kicked off the weeklong celebration chronicled the life of a blues singer who was born and raised in Philly and, after a tumultuous yet successful career, returned here to die. Music buffs and a few high-profile celebrities in designer duds had descended on the City of Brotherly Love, "turning it out" for days afterward.

"That comedian you like. You know he's a big blues fan, so I got a quick interview with him."

"Oh, he's so handsome. He used to drop by my restaurant every now and then."

"Oh, yeah. That's right. His picture with you was on the wall," I said, remembering it with a smile as I absently flicked through the cable channels I hardly ever watched. I settled on a celebrity-gossip channel and pressed mute so I could concentrate on my conversation with Miss Mamie.

"I never could interest him in any of my specialties that weren't on the menu. Not even the girls could get his attention in their heyday," she said with a giggle, referring to her ample bosom, which had always garnered attention from the menfolk, as she called them.

"Miss Mamie," I admonished, "you are so devilish."

She was quiet for a moment before saying, "It's funny

that you'd pick that word. Your momma used to call me that, too."

A soft smile danced on my lips at the mention of my mother. I looked at the sepia-toned portrait of her that sat on my nightstand.

"I still miss her," I said softly.

"Child, you never get over losin' your momma."

My heart already seemed to know that. I closed my eyes and recalled an image of Momma and Miss Mamie laughing heartily, the way they always did when they were together.

"Anybody else I know?" Miss Mamie continued to prod, interrupting my reverie.

I rattled off a few more names, and she responded with oohs and ahhs at those she recognized.

"Okay, baby, it's gettin' late. I know you've got to get to bed so you can get up early for work."

"Yes, ma'am," I drawled. "Have a good night. I'll talk to you tomorrow."

"Okay, little Miss Peach, hang up the line. Had a good talk, but that's the end of your dime."

"Look at Miss Mamie, still rhyming," I commented.

"Until both feet are in the grave. Love you, sweetness."

"Love you back, sugar lump," I said, then hung up the phone.

Talking to Miss Mamie always reconnected me to my southern roots. Although I had lived in Georgia for only seven years, Momma and Miss Mamie had been reared there, Momma in Moultrie and Miss Mamie in Macon. They hadn't known each other there, though. They'd met in Philly when Momma wandered into Miss Mamie's restaurant, and they'd become friends instantly.

Momma had come north after World War II, when the

34

country was opening its arms to the tired, poor, and huddled immigrant masses. She was just a southern transplant, and she let the North Star guide her feet and the Liberty Bell act as her drum. She rented a house in Philly's West Oak Lane because the neighborhood had easy access to Broad Street, the main vein leading to the city's heart. She was titillated by the pulse of the city, and she giggled like a schoolgirl the first time she saw steps leading underground. She told me that she thought it was the shortcut to hell. With her country fearlessness she descended the stairs one morning, and her eyes shone as they beheld the subway, which looked to her like a speeding silver bullet. She slapped down too many coins at the token booth, then boarded the subway, allowing it to whisk her through Olney, Logan, Hunting Park, and North Philly as the train grew more and more crowded. When the subway car slid under City Hall in Center City, Momma was caught in the throng, carried along with the mass of people moving as one as the subway tunnel belched them out.

She had been my jewel, shining even when the light wasn't on her. And the ache of missing her permeated my soul, threatening to unlock buried tears if I thought about her for longer than a few seconds. Glancing at her picture again, I wondered if she would have been proud of what I'd become. Despite some of the scandalous things I'd done, I'd always tried to do right by her.

"God bless you, sweet lady," I said as I plopped down at my vanity table and began removing my makeup. I turned up the volume of the television as the perky host introduced the next segment, in which some young, struggling reporter trying to earn his stripes would dish the dirt on some poor celeb gone astray. I was slathering my hands with Vaseline and preparing to put on my night mittens when I was hit by a blast from the past: "Reporter Randall Myles, who has been camped outside the couple's Malibu home, recovered a note from this trash can . . ."

My jaw dropped in disbelief. Randall had been a respected journalist, nabbing interviews with D.C.'s political power players, and now he was reduced to television's equivalent of a bottom feeder.

Mm-mm-mm.

My mother had always taught me to be gracious. But at that moment, as I remembered how Randall had tried to sabotage me, all grace swirled right down the latrine, and I laughed. This revenge was even better than the downfall I had plotted all those years ago.

Coming into the station at three-thirty one morning to hit the fitness center before work, I sat in the parking lot fumbling around in my purse looking for my key card. Another car pulled in, and I saw Randall hurry out of the building and over to the car, where the driver handed him a small shopping bag. He leaned into the window and kissed the driver on the lips before reaching in to caress the driver's face. When the car passed me on the way to the exit, I clearly saw that the driver was a man. Randall hurried back into the building with the bag, never suspecting that someone had seen him and that his little secret was going to cost him. After all, it was 1990, and America, especially a city as politically conservative as Washington, wasn't ready for a gay anchorman, closeted or otherwise.

Biding my time, I didn't say anything to Randall that day about what I had witnessed. Instead, I found his address and hired a private investigator to get me some dirt. What he brought back to me in a large manila envelope was dirty enough to bury Randall. Picture after picture of him in compromising, unflattering positions were now locked in a safety deposit box at D.C. Federal Bank, and I was willing to use them to my advantage. And I told him so.

"I've been thinking of getting a tattoo," I said to him one morning as my makeup was being applied.

"Oh, yeah," he said, not looking up from his notes.

"But I'm such a crybaby that I'm afraid that I'll just die from the pain," I said, girlishly batting my eyes.

"From what I've heard, it's not that bad," Randall said absently, brushing me off.

"But what about yours?" I asked, feigning innocence. "When you got that heart on your right cheek, or is it your left? You never can tell with photographs. Anyway, did it hurt?"

Randall blanched, his eyes opening wide with surprise. "Get out," he hissed at the makeup artist.

"I know that your friend Timothy just loves it. I could tell by the way he ran his tongue over it on Thursday night."

"Cut the crap, Peach. What do you know?"

"Randall, calm down. They're going to have to put another layer of foundation on you if you don't get your color back before the show."

"I said tell me what you know."

"Isn't it obvious? I know everything. Timothy is a Capitol Hill lobbyist from Dayton, Ohio. You met at a Congressional Black Caucus event three years ago, and you've been living together for the past two years. Before him, there was Pavlos, the gorgeous Greek gym teacher, who you thought was faithful until you busted him in Dupont Circle with a male prostitute. After that, it was just a string of casual yet discreet flings until Timothy came along and swept you off your feet. How's that?"

"My God. What do you want?"

"Nothing. Everything. With our morning show ratings as high as they are, we stand to gain a lot of money from our appearances and more clout here at the station. So I don't have time for your temperamental tantrums. You need to be accessible to me whenever I need you. Got it?"

"And if I don't?"

"You will. D.C. isn't ready for all that . . . uh, stuff. And they'll never know, if you're a good little Randy-Wandy."

He crumpled in his seat as I stood. I applied the last of my lip color before walking to the door. As I looked over my shoulder I saw him wringing his hands.

"Quit the Lady Macbeth routine. Chin up, soldier. Your secret's safe. Unless you decide that you don't want to cooperate," I called over my shoulder before heading out.

That day he was so stiff on the air that Siobhan snapped her fingers at him and said, "Look alive, Randall." After that he pasted a smile on his face, and he was mine.

"How long do we have to stay here?" Randall whined as he slid his car into a space near luxury cars that sparkled despite the dreariness of the winter day. It was The Coterie's quilting exhibit, and I had coaxed Randall into being my date for the afternoon.

"Oh, pep up. Don't be so dour, Randy baby."

"Randall."

"Right, Randy. It should be a nice event, but we won't stay too long. One of my sorors is the chair of the committee that's sponsoring it."

"Are you in The Coterie?"

"Nope."

"Do you want to be?"

"Why, Randy! You actually sound curious about me."

"Oh, forget it. It's not that serious," he said, extending his arm to support me as he helped me out of the car.

Entering the hall, I felt like I was breathing rare air. The guests looked beautiful and relaxed as they circled the room, viewing the handcrafted heirlooms. A harpist played from an invisible location while servers floated about the room offering wine and hors d'oeuvres.

"Here they are, D.C.'s darlings," soror Emma Prescott Daley said as she approached us, looking all shiny and new. I quickly surveyed her from head to toe, taking in her can-that-old-lady-really-walk-in-those-things Italian pumps, gray wool pants, and silk blouse. The outfit was completed by a belted sweater adorned with silver fox tails hanging down the front. She was the picture of class and prosperity, and I was so glad that she had taken a liking to me.

"Hello," I sang-spoke, leaning in for an air kiss. "Of course, you know Randall Myles."

"Who doesn't?" she responded rhetorically. "I'm Emma Prescott Daley. It's a pleasure to meet you."

"The pleasure is mine," he said, kissing her hand.

Emma giggled and blushed like a teenager. "Handsome, successful, and charming. Peach, you sure have got the package with this one."

"Tell me about it," I said, snagging a wine goblet from a server.

"Do you mind if I show him around?"

"Not at all, Soror," I said.

Arm in arm, Emma and Randall dove into the crowd, and

I struck up a conversation with a stockbroker who had a hot tip on an IPO from a clothing company geared toward the growing hip-hop market. He had just handed me his card, and I was feeling great, like this was the life I should have been born into. Cultural events. Affluent, knowledgeable, and influential associates. Insider tips for increasing my wealth. I was thinking that the only thing I was missing was a celebratory cigar. Then I looked up and saw Eve Freeman, the wife of Dr. John Freeman.

There was no ducking, no running away. I was here on equal footing with her, and I wasn't afraid. The past was behind me, and there was nothing I could do to change it. No, I wasn't proud of my actions as far as the Freemans were concerned, but my own silent admission of guilt didn't make looking Eve Freeman in the eye any easier. I'd done what I had to do, and that was that. I'd been foolish enough to hope that she'd understand that, forgive me, and move on. Silly me.

Emma traipsed over to Eve with Randall in tow, and with a cool front that belied the anxiety burning in my chest, I approached the three of them.

"Oh, here comes his other half," Emma was saying as I neared the trio.

"Oh, my God," Eve snorted as she regarded me, but I ignored it, pasting a smile on my face.

Sensing a silent war, glassy-eyed Randall, who had been downing Bombay Sapphires, suddenly looked interested.

"Mrs. Freeman," I said. "What a pleasure seeing you again."

Her eyes shot daggers at me as she quipped, "Too bad I can't say the same."

"You two know each other?" Emma inquired.

"Why, yes. Peach worked under my husband at Moultrie State," she remarked, knowing that I alone understood the double entendre. For clarification, she continued, "He often hires students to work in the administrative offices, answering phones, filing, and doing light typing. Peach worked in that role for some time, and she was a master organizer. She really relieved a lot of his . . . ahem . . . stress," she explained sarcastically.

"But that was a long time ago. It seems like a different life, huh?" she continued. "You're not answering phones anymore."

"She sure isn't," Emma asserted.

"My day wouldn't be nearly as much fun if I didn't begin it with her," Randall said sardonically.

"Mine neither, love," I said, moving closer to his side.

Eve eyed the two of us, locking eyes with Randall. "She is quite a find, isn't she?"

"Yep," he responded, throwing his head back and nearly pouring the last of his fifth drink down his throat.

"You two embarrass me," I said, hoping that no one else caught Randall's sarcasm.

"Aren't you going to ask about Dr. Freeman? You two were so close," Eve said.

"I've kept up on his affairs through the alumni journal, but you can fill me in."

"Well, he's got another student working under him these days, but he hasn't been nearly as organized as he was with you around. Other than that, the word is that Temple's president will be leaving soon, and I've been dying to head back above the Mason-Dixon Line, so I'm trying to work on him. I crave a city with a pulse, and Philadelphia's my home."

"I didn't know that," Emma remarked.

"Peach has been dying to get back there, too. What is it about Philadelphia?" Randall asked.

Eve began blathering on about how Philadelphia is small enough to not get lost in but large enough to have new nooks to be discovered. Trying not to break a sweat, I managed to tune her out until Eve snapped me out of my deliberations, saying, "Randall, let me steal your jewel away for a moment so that we can catch up."

With that, she forcefully scooped me up by the arm and led me toward an empty corner of the hall.

"This life becomes you, Peach. You're looking well, polished and refined. Is that Carolina Herrera you're wearing?"

"It is," I responded blandly with a fake smile on my face. "She's one of my favorite designers."

"That's funny. The girl I knew back in Moultrie didn't have a favorite designer. Her mother made all of her clothes. Isn't it something what a little money and opportunity can do?"

I vacillated between the urge to spit in her face for mentioning my mother in a disrespectful tone and the need to squirm in discomfort as her eyes raked over me.

"Cut to the chase, Eve. What do you want?"

"My, my, Peach. Why so curt? I'm simply making an observation, and you go getting upset. Now, what would happen if I got upset about your actions, huh, dear? Have you thought about that? You're lucky that I'm a forgiving woman, Peach."

"Eve, I don't have the time or the tolerance for your bullshit. Besides, it's not like you really wanted him anyway."

Her eyes flashed as she recognized that I knew her secret.

"You don't mess with what's mine," she retorted.

"Whatever, Eve. Now, if you have something real to say to me, say it. If not, I have to get back to my fiancé."

"Fiancé? I don't see a ring. Besides, I know a beard when I see one."

"Excuse me?"

"Come on, Peach. He's as gay as the day is long. Don't you think that I, of all people, know a front when I see one?"

"I don't know what you're talking about."

"Sure, you do. What's the deal? Why are you holding on to him? Or is he holding on to you?"

"I have to go," I said, preparing to walk away.

"If you walk away from me, you'll regret it."

My head snapped around to her, and all of the urban edge that I had repressed for decades came bubbling to the surface. "Look, Eve. You have no hold on me. In case you haven't noticed, these people love me. Look at them," I said, gesturing toward the crowd of people, some of whom were peeking at me inconspicuously. "I'm D.C.'s darling, and there's nothing you can do to me," I hissed angrily.

I straightened my shoulders and began to walk away, furious at myself for allowing her to get my goat. I was pleased, though, because I felt empowered. She and John Freeman were in my history, but I had my present, which I was loving, and I had my whole future ahead of me.

"Don't say that I didn't warn you," Eve said to my back.

I brushed her off with a diva's toss of the hair and continued strutting away. As I headed toward the ladies' room to collect myself I felt pride surge through me. A weaker person would have been scampering out the door, too flustered by the confrontation to enjoy the rest of the event. Not Peach Harrison. After powdering my nose, I went to catch up with

Randall, whose eyes had glazed over after too many drinks and too many introductions by Emma.

"Are you ready?" he slurred. He looked sad, and I felt a little bit sorry for him.

"Give me fifteen more minutes to work the room. Then I'll let you drop me off and head home to Timothy. Okay?" I whispered.

He sniffed and nodded, looking like a little boy promising to be good in order to receive a treat later on. It was a look that made me consider calling everything off, disposing of the incriminating photos, staying in D.C. and working in my current job like an honest woman, and forgetting about the hurt and shame of my childhood. That last thing would be the most difficult to do, but it was the most important. It was the thing that was fueling my rage, and I had no right to take it out on Randall or anyone else. Looking at Randall, I smiled a genuine smile, and he reciprocated.

I made the rounds quickly, posing for a few press photos and saying my good-byes. Before long, Randall and I were back in his car, heading for my town house. After he dropped me off, I drew a hot bath and perched myself on the edge of the tub where I did something that I hadn't done in a long time. I prayed. I prayed for cleansing and wholeness and healing. I prayed for forgiveness and the ability to forgive. I knew that revenge was wrong and that I shouldn't hold on to those feelings, but I'd found it so hard to let go. I tried to remember that God said, "Vengeance is mine." I just wanted to be made new and free from the torturous memories that twisted my mind and corrupted my actions, so as I immersed myself in the tub, I thought of baptism and rebirth. I imagined the tub in my town house as the River Jordan, but I was my own John the Baptist.

Upon exiting the tub, I went into the bedroom and rummaged through the drawer in my nightstand, looking for the Bible that Momma had given me when I graduated from Moultrie High School. Not knowing where to start, I just opened the book, and the leaves fell open to the book of Joshua. I didn't fully comprehend what I read, but the passage that my eyes fell on was about a harlot named Rahab, who was in the bloodline of Jesus. Stories of sinners who got saved excited me, because they made me feel that there was hope for me. Rahab, who had given shelter to two spies, was spared the wrath of Joshua, his army, and God when everyone else within the walls of Jericho perished. I wasn't asking God to smite my enemies, whatever *smite* meant anyway, but I wanted redemption. I wanted to feel what it must have felt like to be chosen, to be spared, to be that special, and to be filled up by that special feeling. So I thought about it and prayed about it, and I realized that no matter how much dirt I had done, Rahab had done more. Yet still she was spared. That thought filled me with a warmth that permeated through me, hallowing my soul.

And lasted for about two days.

I knew that Randall was up to something when he came in on Wednesday grinning like the Cheshire cat who swallowed the canary. Ready to wage war on my newly sanctified self.

"I ran into a classmate from Hampton the other day, and we had a good time reminiscing about old traditions that the students still have," he said with a smile, temporarily lost in his memories.

"One of them deals with this patch of grass in front of Ogden Hall. Oh, Ogden Hall is a concert hall that's a National Historic Landmark," he explained. "Did you all have any national landmarks at Moultrie State?"

"I'm not sure. Most of us weren't interested in stuff like that," I sputtered, caught off guard.

He rolled his eyes and continued: "Well, anyway, no one was allowed to step on the grass in front of Ogden Hall—Ogden Circle, it was called—until the night before graduation, after the singing of the alma mater. It was probably something the administration cooked up to keep us from ruining the landscaping, but we all went along with it. All except the occasional renegade freshman with no esprit de corps. You know?"

Randall's eyes glazed over as he remembered the school that he often called his "home by the sea."

"Ooh, and there's another one. Instead of doing it by year, Hamptonians often identify themselves by class name. Each year the seniors try to get the incoming freshman class to adopt their class name. They're names like Onyx, Quintessence, Ogre Phi Ogre, and Dynasty. It's all in fun, but it's really a big deal, too. T-shirts with the class name. Homecoming floats. I was Onyx," he announced proudly, as if it made a difference to me.

"What about you guys?" he asked with a gleam in his eye.

"No, we didn't do the class-name thing," I replied coolly, looking over my notes for the morning's news. Clearly he was up to something, but at the time I couldn't put my finger on it.

"Did you have a lot of student loans to pay off after graduation?" he asked, touching a raw nerve without understanding why.

"No," I snapped angrily. "My mother worked her fingers to the bone to pay for my education, and she died before she got to see me graduate. I picked up where she left off, so I left Moultrie State without owing a thing to anyone. Does that satisfy you, Randall?"

He simply smiled while the makeup artist finished prepping him, and I again wondered why all the questions about my college experience.

After the early morning news, I went to call Miss Mamie for our weekly gossip ritual.

"And the senator said what?" Miss Mamie shrieked as I filled her in on D.C.'s juicy secrets.

"You heard me right," I said, looking up just in time to see Randall pass by my office on his way to his own.

We chatted for a few more minutes before I hung up and headed for his office. I wanted to find out why he was suddenly so curious about my educational experiences.

I softened my steps as I approached his door, which was partially open. His voice was low, but I could still make out what he was saying: "No, she wouldn't bite. . . . Why don't you just tell me? . . . She's too manipulative for that. . . . Uh-hunh . . . okay . . . I can't wait to find out. Okay, I'll see you at six, Eve."

My palms began to burn as I stood frozen in the hallway. I couldn't believe that Eve would stoop so low as to rehash that old dirt from my college days. She couldn't possibly hurt me now, since I was already set in my career, but Randall obviously thought that this juvenile, insignificant bit of gossip was equal to the dirt that I had on him. And now he was going to try playing tit for tat. I'd told him to just cooperate with me and everything would be fine, but he had to try his luck. Now he was going to suffer.

He was smug as he reported the midday news. I, on the other hand, continued to play the doting role of half of D.C.'s darling couple. After work I tore out of the station heading directly for the safety deposit box at D.C. Federal Bank, where I'd stashed the compromising photos of Randall. I went home, washed off my makeup, and exchanged my designer duds for something less conspicuous. I grabbed some large yellow envelopes from my home office and addressed them to every mainstream and niche newspaper in the area before enclosing a photo in each. Then I grabbed my car keys and my bundle of envelopes and rushed out the door.

Once downtown, I found a courier who had just finished making his deliveries. I slipped him $500, handed him the envelopes, and sent him on his way to the newspapers. When I returned home, I placed a phone call to a gourmet grocery store in Georgetown and ordered a dozen doughnut peaches with a side of cream, asking that they be delivered to Randall's house that evening. Then I sat back, turned on the television, and waited for the shit to hit the fan.

By eight o'clock, my phone was ringing off the hook with calls from my NABJ associates at news outlets around the city. I let the machine take all of the calls except one. The one that I took was from Rachel Kane, D.C.'s biggest gossip. I fake-sobbed on the phone in her ear, making myself look like a martyr, sure that the story of my heartbreak would hit the underground grapevine like greased lightning. After talking to her, I sat back and watched the tornado gain momentum on every station. At eleven o'clock all of the stations were abuzz.

"Breaking news from our newsroom. KDC's television anchor Randall Myles is said to be in hiding after photos . . ."

"This just in. Half of the daybreak duo known as D.C.'s darlings has some explaining to do. While they are too explicit to be shown here, some unflattering photographs . . ."

"Reporting live from outside the residence that news anchor Randall Myles is said to occupy with this man . . ."

After making sure that the story was covered on every channel, I turned off the television and went to sleep for the next four hours without a tinge of guilt.

The next morning I arrived at the station, looking appropriately haggard, and I did a lackluster job of reporting the news. Solo. After the midday installment, my general manager called me into his office, where he gave me his condolences and told me to take as much time off as I needed.

"Jack, I don't think I can come back," I said with fake tears collecting in the corners of my eyes.

"I understand that. On the other hand, we've got your contract to consider, but I'll speak to legal and see what we can do. In the meantime, let me make a few calls to friends at a couple of stations on the East Coast to check out some other possibilities for you. Call me in a couple of days."

"Okay," I sniffled.

"And Peach. Out of concern for you, let me be blunt: Get yourself checked out with your doctor. There's no telling what that scoundrel may have exposed you to."

I looked at my hands and willed an onslaught of tears to fall. On cue, Jack moved in to console me. I put up my hand to let him know that it wasn't necessary, but I shuddered once more for good measure. I stood and headed for the door, wiping my eyes dramatically one last time.

Jack called me the next week with the best news yet: A position was opening up in Philly. I couldn't have been more thrilled. I'd always thrived under pressure, and this was definitely a tense time. In a matter of weeks I'd be back in the city, and boy, would I take it by storm.

3

There are some fabrics that look exactly as they are: delicate or sturdy, fine or durable. I prided myself on knowing the difference between them. For instance, I knew that brocade, a heavy fabric used in everything from upholstery and curtains to gowns and outer coats, was durable yet still beautiful. Velvet was deceptive. To the eye, it appeared soft and inviting, and nothing was more elegant than black velvet. Yet when flipped on its reverse side, velvet was no more inviting than a burlap sack.

That's exactly the way Randall Myles had been. He'd seemed mild enough, but he'd tried to cross me, using what he thought was ammunition from Eve Freeman, but his plan had backfired.

What Eve had been ready to tell Randall was that I hadn't earned my degree from Moultrie State legitimately. That I'd resorted to the world's oldest profession, prostituting myself to her husband, to get it. And I suppose that Randall would have tried to use that information to embarrass me. Maybe even on the air. But they were both wrong. You see, I hadn't gotten the degree by working on my back. It was acquired just as any other student had obtained a degree: lots of studying, burning the midnight oil, the usual routine. Only I'd had to pay for my senior year by cleaning *and* doing extra work on my back and on my knees and any other way that John Freeman wanted me. Officially and for the record, I'd been granted a scholarship due to my special circumstances. No one needed to know that John Freeman was my benefactor.

Momma had died at the end of my junior year, and I'd had every intention of finishing my college degree, as she'd wanted me to. She'd saved a little, but it wasn't enough to pay for my schooling. So shortly after she died, I went to the financial aid office to apply. Momma would have been angry at me for doing that, because she was a proud woman who didn't want any part of anything that looked like charity. My choices were limited, though. It was either apply for financial aid and deal with the loans after graduation or change my status from full-time to part-time student and finish the degree by taking one class at a time. My pride wouldn't allow me to finish my education in such a piecemeal fashion.

I opened the envelope containing details about my work-study assignment, and it was enough to stop me in my tracks. Domestic engineering? Domestic engineering! Housekeeping! Here I was, the northern-born daughter of a southern-born domestic who had escaped the South in hopes of achieving a dream that would permanently remove the family line from the service industry. Yet Momma had been run out of Philadelphia, only to return to her southern homeland with a highly polished, poised, and well-spoken daughter who ends up cleaning toilets in a women's dorm. When I got the assignment, I laughed so hard at the irony of it that I cried.

Working at Moultrie State wasn't as terrible as I expected it would be. But it wasn't great either. I wasn't as community minded as my mother, who could look at other blacks, even those who held her at arm's length, and applaud their accomplishments. People are born with different temperaments, but I was born with the tenacity to succeed. If that was rewarded, I'd have been much further along than I was. I had been waiting my turn to rise to the top like the cream of the crop, but my lot was different. I looked at the other Moultrie State girls, and I could feel the bitter gall swirling in my stomach. I refused to let it creep up and seep out, but I still knew it was there. I found consolation in the hope that my situation was temporary. It was the summer session, so there weren't many witnesses to my humiliation. Besides, at least this wasn't Spelman, Hampton, or Howard. I'd never be able to stomach being in such privileged company in my humbled state.

Picking tufts of hair from the drains of the showers in the communal bathrooms. Scraping dried clumps of white and turquoise toothpaste from the porcelain sinks. Holding my nose as I poured a bleach solution into the commode before I scraped away the streaks of dried feces spattered around the lip. I was in the pit of despair, but for dignity's sake I kept my shoulders squared instead of hunched over. Even as I watched the inconsiderate residents of the dorm traipse carelessly over the hallway I had just mopped, leaving dirty footsteps in their wake.

Among the things I had learned while living in Philly was to keep my ears open at all times. Like the slaves who silently waited on the family at dinner in the big house, I had picked up tons of valuable information that way. Working among the students at Moultrie State was no different. Their conversations were like bread and air to me. I listened to the students talk about what works they were reading in their classes. I heard them discuss the implications of the upcoming presidential election. I took in all of the business tips they tossed back and forth. I listened as they talked about the college's administration, especially the president, Dr. John A. Freeman, who they all agreed was fine, in that subtle Morris Chestnut way. I tuned in to their discussions about sorority life, and I recognized the name of one of the organizations. It was the sorority to which Eliza, Elizabeth, and Louise, my mother's former employers in Philadelphia, belonged.

From the snatches of conversation that I heard, more than a few students were interested in pledging Delta Alpha Zeta Sorority. They spoke in hushed tones behind their doors, whispering about how thorough Big Sister So-and-So is and how four of the Big Six accounting firms were courting Big Sister Such-a-One because she is so impressive. They rattled off names of prominent sorors of Dazzling Delta Alpha Zeta and murmured their wishes to be counted among the number of that sisterhood. They whispered about how rarely that chapter did membership intake, but the word about campus was that there would be a membership rush in the fall semester, not that I'd be able to join now. Membership was expensive, and as a student I'd never be able to afford it no matter how desperately I wanted to join so that I could be counted among the elite. Like Eliza and her daughters.

They had been presented to Philadelphia society through Eliza's membership in the selective social and service organization. Their induction into that world had been certain, simply based on lineage. I wanted the same thing, but my lack of preparation for such a place in society prohibited my belonging. But I wanted to belong. I needed to belong. My desire was much bigger than the sorority. It was rooted in my need for validation. In my eyes, such validation could come only through pledging Delta Alpha Zeta Sorority, Incorporated.

Since my arrival on campus, I had watched the periodic growth in membership numbers. Unlike the other sororities, which had at least one line of pledges per year, provided that they weren't suspended from operating on campus for a semester, Delta Alpha Zeta took on a line only once every two years. When the first line was being made, I attended the rush. I absorbed all of the general information that the sorors presented, and when some of the girls from the dorm I used to clean were accepted into the sisterhood, they met for information and study sessions in their dorm rooms. I lapped up every syllable, knowing that the secrets they whispered behind closed doors would be part of my entrée to a new world.

When the second line was being made, I visited the school store and purchased sorority paraphernalia, which included umbrellas, key chains, tote bags, and polo-style shirts. It was frowned upon for a non-Greek to purchase such paraphernalia unless it was a gift for a member. I didn't care. I purchased it anyway. It was also taboo for a nonmember to wear anything that contained the sacred Greek letters Delta Alpha Zeta. I didn't care about that either. I longed to be able to claim membership publicly now, but at that point it looked as if I'd never be able to.

After my two-month initial probation period for work was over, I got a raise and word that I had been reassigned. My new detail was to clean the administration building, which included the offices of the deans, the vice presidents, the registrar, and the president, Dr. John A. Freeman.

Every afternoon after class, I punched in at four-fifteen. After listening to my coworkers shoot the breeze and thumbing through a copy of Moultrie's newspaper, I left the custodians' lounge and made my way toward the A Building, as my post was called. Once there, I unlocked the door that held my cleaning supplies and wheeled my cart out of the closet. After plugging in my radio and tape player, I popped in one of the jazz tapes that served as background music for my reveries as I worked. George Howard, Freddie Hubbard, Miles Davis, or John Coltrane would drift through the air as I cleaned the first floor.

First I cleaned the student-accounts suite, emptying the trash cans, wiping down the counters, and polishing the wooden counter on which students leaned while waiting to be helped. I mopped the floor before taking the elevator to the second floor, where I perched my radio on the windowsill at the end of the hall, then unlocked all of the offices and opened the doors before I took a break.

Each day, when I was sure that no one was around, I chose one of the administrators' offices and sat there, imagining what their lives were like. I studied the framed degrees that decorated the walls. I looked at the pictures on their desks, admiring their happy, stable families. I checked their datebooks, wondering about the engagements they had penciled into their calendars, and I thought of how important they must feel.

"Good morning. I'm Dr. Violet Anderson," I'd say, smiling,

talking to the air. I'd pronounce the miscellaneous names with pride and confidence, hoping that one day I'd be able to say my own name with such pride and dignity.

After cleaning the second floor, I walked back to the custodians' lounge, where I ate dinner and got some of my reading done for class. As darkness crept over the campus I made my way back to the A Building, where I prepared to clean the third floor.

Dr. Freeman's was the lone office up there, but there was also a Xerox room, a storage room, and a break room. They needed relatively little care. Dr. Freeman's office, on the other hand, required a more thorough touch.

Beginning with the reception area, the president's quarters were a delight for the senses. The walls were dark wood with brass fixtures that contrasted with the somberness of the décor. Framed limited-edition prints hung on the walls above plush chairs and loveseats. Travel and business magazines dotted coffee and end tables, while fleshy succulent plants reached out from the corners of the room. The reception area exuded an elegance that I missed. It was like Philadelphia for me, and I savored every moment in it.

Dr. Freeman's outer office, where he held meetings and interviews, was as rich as that of the reception area. His degrees hung on the wall behind his desk, and photographs of him with politicians, authors, and artists adorned the wall near the bar. A collection of cigars sat in a humidor on a stand near the doors to the balcony, which overlooked the campus.

His inner office was the place where he worked, and though it was intimate, it lacked none of the richness of the other rooms. The office contained a closet, where he always kept three suits, extra shirts starched to crispness, and Italian leather shoes. The office also held a private bath, complete with a shower, a shaving chair, and a massage table. In addition, there was a private entrance, which I supposed he used when he preferred privacy. The office was decorated in a minimalist style, leaving little room for distraction. At least that's what he told me when I first met him.

That night I had cleaned the Xerox and break rooms and was lingering over the reception area and the outer office as I usually did. Taking my time and enjoying these rooms while thumbing through the business and travel magazines planted seeds of happy dreams in my mind, giving me hope for what I sought to achieve one day. I approached the door to the inner office, humming to Ella Fitzgerald, whom I considered to have the most beautiful voice of all time. After I slid my key in the lock, I expected the door to give as it usually did, but it did not. I tried again, but the door still didn't yield. I heard footsteps approach from the other side, and when the door opened, there stood Dr. Freeman, looking tired but amused.

"So you're a jazz lover, huh? A little young to appreciate Ella."

"Pardon me. I didn't realize that anyone was still here," I replied, avoiding being obsequious although embarrassment filled me.

"It's okay. I'll be out of your way shortly."

"Don't rush. I have other—" I started, backing out of the door.

"No, stay. I'm really on my way out," he said, moving behind his desk. He motioned for me to have a seat while he began straightening the papers that were strewn across the desk.

"Booker T. Washington, the Wizard of Tuskegee Institute,

said you should always clear your desk before leaving work. Clutter creates chaos," he said, looking around the orderly office.

"Washington also said that vacations are for the lazy," I commented.

"Not quite, but I'm glad that you've read *Up from Slavery*. A jazz lover and a bibliophile. Impressive," he remarked, putting on his blazer.

"It's good to be well-rounded."

"You're right, young lady. Absolutely right." He moved toward the door to the private exit. "Have a good evening," he said, smiling.

"Good night," I responded, leaning against the wall across from his desk.

"He certainly is charming, and those students weren't lying when they said that he's fine," I thought, heading for my cart so I could clean this last room before punching out and going home.

For the next month, at least twice a week when I came in to clean his inner office, a jazz tape or a book, mostly the black classics, was left perched on the corner of the desk. On top of each item was an engraved piece of card stock with my name, Claudia Fryar, scrawled on it. I hadn't told him my name, so I was flattered that he had inquired about me. Each time I simply turned the card over, wrote "Thank you" on the reverse, and left it on his desk.

More often, I began to see him working late in his office.

Besides the occasional light conversation, our exchanges were professional, although I suspected that if I gave any indication that I wanted something more, he would be game. One night I gave the signal, and he took the bait like a piranha.

I was taking a break on the third floor, sitting at the receptionist's desk and poring over a paper I was revising for English 102, when Dr. Freeman came out of his office and spoke to me.

"No music tonight, huh? You must be hard at work."

"Sure am. How did you know?"

"You're a creature of habit, and I've gotten to know a lot about you and your habits."

"Like what, Dr. Freeman? Tell me about myself," I said, leaning back in my chair.

He came closer and sat on the desk in front of me.

"Well, let's see. You're not from here, but you have southern roots. You were educated up north somewhere, right?"

"Philadelphia," I said, nodding.

"Prep school, I'd say, because of your carriage and speech," he ventured.

I smiled. If living under the heel of Philadelphia's elite hadn't been preparation in refinement for life, I didn't know what was. "Sort of," I responded.

"You're intelligent, and you're young, but you're working full time in addition to carrying a full load of courses, which, judging from your demeanor, is a big change for you. Not that you're not a hard worker. This just seems a bit beneath you."

I lowered my eyes, unsure of what to reveal. After clearing my throat and squaring my shoulders, sidestepping victimhood, I replied simply, "My mother wanted to return to her hometown." Then I looked into his eyes.

"How long do you plan to work here?"

"You're supposed to know that, too, aren't you?" I said with a faint smile on my lips.

He smiled and loosened his tie. "Touché. Well, truthfully, I don't think that you'll be here long. You're ambitious and intelligent, and you can do more than empty trash cans."

I smiled, letting his compliment sink in. Lowering my lashes coyly as I had seen Miss Mamie do, I paused before speaking. "Before I came here, I interned at a radio station. I worked with the News and Public Affairs Director, and I was pretty much a gofer. One night he was stuck in traffic and couldn't get back to the station in time, so I had to do his show solo. It was one of the best experiences of my life." I paused to savor the memory.

"Have you ever thought about television?" Dr. Freeman inquired.

"It's crossed my mind," I responded casually, knowing that it truly was my ultimate goal.

"You should really consider it. You've got the look for it."

Again borrowing a page from Miss Mamie, I looked at him doe-eyed. After years of waiting to "grow into" my beauty, I wasn't used to receiving compliments, but I didn't let on that it was new to me.

"What do you mean?" I asked, wanting to draw him out to see where he stood.

"I think you know," he said, grinning.

"Say it," I said, standing and walking from the reception- ist area into his outer office. He followed me, entering the room and locking the door behind him.

"You're beautiful," he revealed, leaning against the door.

I planted myself between his legs, smelling the mint on his breath.

"You think so?" I asked breathily.

"I've always thought so."

"So why didn't you say so?"

"I have to be careful. I'm a married man, and I've got a reputation to maintain."

"Sometimes you've got to go with your gut, though."

As he wrapped his arms around my waist he questioned me rhetorically. "Oh, yeah?"

"Un-hunh," I responded, stepping into his warmth.

Before another thought could pass through my mind, his lips were pressed on mine. They were soft, and when his mouth opened, his tongue filled my mouth with a sweetness that was breathtaking.

The kiss was over too soon. As I leaned away to look at him he smiled and said, "Your kiss is as sweet as a Georgia peach. That's what I'll call you. Peach."

4

Dr. John Freeman was like polyester. Not the 1970s, cheesy-looking kind that would go up in flames if one ventured near a fireplace or even a cigarette lighter. He was more like the newer, hipper, stylish polyester. The kind that was nice-looking, reliable, and versatile. He was all of those things to me, and I regarded him with almost worshipful reverence.

He took care of the cost of my tuition for the rest of my senior year, so I was able to fully immerse myself in my studies again, though, for appearance's sake, I had to show up at his office as if I was working as his assistant for the scholarship he was giving me. The financial pressure was lifted like a weight off of my shoulders, and for that I was grateful but not completely relieved. He was my patron of sorts, so I granted him free access to me whenever he wanted. My youthful innocence and energy invigorated him, and he doted on me in a paternalistic manner, taking great joy in teaching me various things like how to play poker, how to mix drinks, and how to give a perfect blow job.

I accepted gifts from him that included a ruby bracelet, tickets to plays and jazz concerts, perfumes, handbags, jewelry, and, of course, everyone's favorite, cash. I used it to pay bills and to get myself a nice little used car to get around in. For years I had ridden my bike to and from campus, which had whittled my waist down to a perfect size four. Now it was time for me to have a little comfort.

The thought did occur to me that I was selling myself. In my active, alert hours I brushed that thought aside, and it was easy to do so. After all, I'd lived a hard life, and I deserved nice things. At least I deserved them as much as the Harrisons did. My mother worked harder than Eliza Harrison ever had, but she still struggled while Eliza never had to concern herself with financial issues. Our situations proved that merit didn't always have a relationship to comfort. Familial connection, not hard work, was the thing that had made Elizabeth, Louis, and their daughters' lives so comfortable while my own, as it stood then, was rough by comparison. So what if John Freeman was married and supposed to be off-limits. I hadn't had anyone to spoil me all those years, so now if I had to spend a little extra time on my back or on my knees to get some of the things I wanted, so be it. At least there was a modicum of security in my situation. His reputation and marriage had to be maintained, protected even, so I felt somewhat safe even though my safety stemmed from manipulation and latent but easily accessible potential threats of blackmail.

"What do you want from me?" he asked after our first sexual encounter.

I simply smiled as I walked into his private bathroom and opened the linen closet for a washcloth. He followed me in, and standing behind me as I gazed at my image in the mirror, he leaned down and kissed my naked shoulder. His bare body, still surprisingly firm and fit for his age, gave off a fire-like warmth.

"Peach, I'm serious. What do you want from me? I'm an old man. I'm forty-five. What's that, double your age?"

"I'm twenty. You're more than double my age," I teased, correcting him.

"Good grief. I'm more than robbing the cradle," he lamented, leaning back against the smoky gray tile of the bathroom. "Really, what could you possibly want from me?"

I lowered my head, collecting my thoughts and feigning a show of emotion.

"I don't really know. It sounds so juvenile, but I like you. I actually admire you. Not just for your accomplishments, but for the way you conduct your affairs. In my heart of hearts, I also can't help but feel that it's some sort of unresolved paternal conflict. Or it could be a simple crush like most girls get when they are in the company of powerful men. Whatever it is"—I paused dramatically for effect—"it's real. You were my first, so now you're stuck with me, at least until you get tired of me. So to answer your question, what I want from you is anything that you can give me. And I hope it's your best."

When I finished speaking, I looked back up and into the mirror, zeroing in on his eyes. They twinkled as he smiled at me. Then he came toward me, lifting me up and carrying me into the shower, where the heat of our bodies, coupled with the warmth of the water, steamed up the walls of the glass stall.

The next day I received my first pair of diamond earrings.

As good as things were, I knew not to expect too much. He was married, and I couldn't forget that. Especially when I saw Mrs. Freeman on his arm. I didn't see them much, just as they rushed to the occasional dinner for the Board of Trustees or the opening reception for a new exhibit at the art museum on campus or another function where decorum made their joint presence necessary. When I did see them together, it served to remind me of the impermanence of things. Reality kicked in, and I remembered that it wasn't really a relationship but merely an arrangement, with both of us gaining something. Realistically I knew that, but Eve Freeman's arrival at his office one evening reminded me.

We had been in his outer office laughing as he taught me how to putt on the little artificial strip of green that he kept there for practice. I heard her footsteps before he did, and that gave me enough time to scurry across the room to pick up a notepad.

"Dr. Freeman," I said, clearing my throat, "maybe your game will improve by the time I finish typing these recommendations for you."

He noted the change in my demeanor, and he straightened up as well.

"Hi, dear," Mrs. Freeman said, gliding across the office to kiss her husband.

I don't know if I expected him to be flustered, but clearly he wasn't, for he reciprocated without batting an eye. I collected my things, waiting for an audible sign indicating that she knew that they weren't alone. It didn't come, either because she didn't see me or because she was ignoring me. I chose to believe the former.

"I just got off the phone with Margaret Howell, my Coterie sister from Philadelphia, and she updated me on the planning meeting for the national convention. We were able to get into the Mountainside Inn in the Poconos for this weekend. I know that it's last-minute, but would it be a problem if I went?"

"Not at all. You know that there is always work for me to do. I'll miss you, though."

"Oh, you sweet thing. Here, let me call Margaret," she said, floating toward the desk and picking up the phone.

Standing with the handset pressed to her ear, she finally nodded in my direction. I responded with a nod and peeled my eyes from her, although it was difficult to do. She was beautiful and elegant, with a dancer's posture and a model's waistline. Her skin was the color of sand, not washed-out white sand from an island but Rehoboth Beach sand, tan and subtle. A mane of loosely curled dark brown hair flowed away from her face, and her chocolate, almond-shaped eyes stayed on me as she spoke into the receiver.

"Wow," I thought. "If he has her, what does he want from me?" I was attractive, I knew, but she was the package. She was what I would be, once I truly got myself on the path.

I moved toward the door as the room filled with her chatter. John continued putting, seeming completely undisturbed by the presence of his two lovers.

When Mrs. Freeman hung up, she turned to her husband. "Okay, honey, I need to go pick up a few things. I should be home by nine."

"Alright," he responded, leaning down to deliver a peck on her expectant cheek.

On her way out she again turned her attention to me. "Hello, young lady. I'm Eve Freeman," she said, extending her hand and pulling me close to her.

"Mrs. Freeman, I'm Claudia Fryar."

"Nice meeting you, dear," she said. She leaned toward me as if she were about to confide a secret, but just as quickly she withdrew.

"Smells familiar," she whispered before drifting out of the door, and I was momentarily startled by her comment, wondering what she knew.

"She's very pretty," I commented when she was out of earshot.

"Yeah, she's something else," he responded, putting his putter in the corner and grabbing his suit jacket from behind the door. We left his office through the private exit, and he drove me to my car, kissing me quickly before I got out.

The weekend found us in a cabin hideaway that he owned in north Florida, where we played hard during the day and even harder at night. After a day of fishing, on Saturday night we lounged in the living room between lovemaking sessions, waiting for the freshly caught fish and some ears of corn to roast in the fireplace. The orange glow from the fire cast the room in a romantic amber hue while the vocal stylings of Sarah Vaughan poured from the speakers. Sitting on the sofa, I sipped the Shiraz that he poured while he tended to the fire.

"John, this is beautiful. I'm having a great time," I commented.

When he turned from the fire, I was surprised to find myself wishing that this thing we had was real. "I could love a man like him," I mused briefly before shaking the thought from my head. Yeah, right. A man like him, gorgeous, successful, and comfortable, was hidden away in a cabin with me while his wife was hundreds of miles away.

He smiled before asking, "What was that all about?"

"I was just thinking, why am I here?"

"You just said that you were having a great time. I hope that's why you're here."

Setting my goblet on the coffee table, I asked more directly, "No, I mean, what are we doing? You've got a fabulous life with a beautiful wife. So why am I here with you, taking your wife's place?"

He looked down, knitting his eyebrows before speaking. "You aren't taking her place. No one can. But things aren't always as they seem, Peach."

"Explain what that means," I said softly, patting the sofa and inviting him to sit next to me.

"My wife is truly special to me, and I love her. She loves me, too, but . . . I can't do anything for her."

I waited quietly for him to continue. As he settled back onto the sofa he tried to relax while unfolding a tale that was anything but soothing.

"Eve was a first-semester junior at Penn when I met her. I was teaching her sociology class, and she would come in every day and perch herself right in the front row. She knew that I noticed her. Women always know those things. I was certainly a sight. Thick glasses, dead wardrobe, jacked-up haircut. Anyway, she must have taken pity on me, the lowly assistant professor, because on the first day of the spring semester, after her class with me had ended, she showed up in my office with a stack of *GQ* and *Ebony Man* magazines. We spent the semester doing an exchange. She would pick my brain about sociological subjects, and I would benefit from her sense of style. By summer she had the outside of me groomed to perfection, so she began working on building me up professionally and socially.

"She was like a muse, encouraging me to submit articles for publication and the other things I needed to do to attract the attention I needed to obtain full professor status. By the end of her fourth year, I had done it, and I owed it all to her, a student. I was truly grateful, and I wanted to do something nice for her. So I took her out to dinner.

"Everything about it felt so easy to me. She was laid-back, and she didn't pressure me. If I didn't call when I said I would, she didn't try to castrate me. She simply inspired me without pushing or nagging, and when the department-chair position opened up, she not only prompted me to apply, but she courted and schmoozed all the right people, some of whom happened to be friends of her family, who were Penn alums and very connected and influential. And I got the position. A few years later a position opened up at UVA, for the dean of the College of Liberal Arts. They were advertising heavily in *Black Issues in Higher Education*, trying to find someone of color for the position. I got that, too. Everything just seemed to be falling in line, but something was missing. I needed a partner, and I wanted it to be her.

"When I asked her to marry me, tears filled her eyes. She said, 'There's so much that you don't know about me.' I told her that if I didn't know by now, I didn't need to know. We had a quick ceremony, and we left for Charlottesville the next day. On our wedding night I thought our rhythm was off because of the haste of things. But even when we got settled in Charlottesville, things didn't improve in the bedroom. Meanwhile, everything else was perfect. She was joining various social organizations and making good connections for us. All I had to do was just show up for things, because she was the master social planner. Life seemed pretty good, but I soon learned that ignorance is bliss."

He took a deep breath before filling his mouth with Shiraz. He swished it around in his cheeks. He stood up to peek in the foil at the fish and corn. "If I had known that I'd be talking about this, I would have brought some brandy—anything harder than wine," he said, giving a half smile.

"I walked in one day. It was like the proverbial husband-coming-home-for-lunch scenario . . . only she wasn't with another man."

"What did you do?"

"I backed out of the bedroom, went downstairs to the living room, and waited. They came downstairs, and the woman went out the door. Eve sat across from me, wringing her hands. She wouldn't cry, but her eyes looked sad."

He paused, pouring another glass and gulping it before continuing. "She said, 'I told you there were things you didn't know about me, and you told me you didn't care. This is who I am. It's who I've always been. I love you, and I want to be a good wife to you, but you have to know that this is me. I'll be discreet, I promise you, but . . .' I didn't want to listen to any more. Who wanted a wife who was . . . ? So I got up and left. I guess part of me had known all along, but I ignored my gut. I stayed out late that night, thinking and drinking, trying to sort things out. I was hurt, but I loved her. She had done so much for me. She had been my rock, and she had never asked for anything in return. She never wanted anything from me."

"So what happened?" I asked, anxious to know how he'd resolved the issue.

"I decided to go home to her. I stopped at a convenience store and picked out the best flowers they had. They were pretty pitiful, and that's how I must have looked when I rang the doorbell. I didn't want to chance walking in on anything again. She opened the door with tears in her eyes, and she reached out to me. And I held her. And I've been holding her ever since."

"So basically, you let her do her thing, and you do your own?"

"That's about right. But we always try to be discreet when we're fulfilling our needs."

"So I'm here to fulfill your needs?"

"Well, yeah, but we're having fun together, right?"

"Yeah," I responded. His question focused me on something that had been on my mind. "We're having fun."

I leaned over to kiss him as he was scooting to the end of the sofa, getting up to retrieve the food from the fireplace. As he stooped before the hearth I thought about my future. I knew that I was a temporary source of fun for him, and that he wouldn't be around for much longer to supply the support that he had been giving me thus far. Before he kicked me to the curb, I needed him to do something for me.

I was a senior, and I had no contacts to help me break into my field. Since leaving Philly, I'd had no internships to boost my résumé. My summers had been spent simply working at whatever jobs paid well so I could contribute something to the pot. So now here I stood, about to strike out in the world but without a real plan.

"There's something I'd like from you," I said to him on the ride home.

"Okay," he replied. I'd learned enough about him to know that he wasn't consenting. He was simply agreeing to hear my request.

"I'll be graduating in May, and it seems that I don't have a place to start. I know that powerful men run in powerful circles, so I was wondering if you have any contacts in mass media that I could use."

He looked at me soberly, and I could tell he was thinking that my plan all along had been to use him for what he could do for me. I slid my hand over to his thigh, massaging gently, hoping to remove the thought from his mind. He patted my hand before responding.

"Sure, Peach. One of my associates is the general manager of a television station in Atlanta. I'll give you his number, but I'll give him a call first as a heads-up."

"Thanks, John," I said, nestling closer to him.

He caressed my hair gently before guiding my head toward his lap, and I pleasured him as we rode back toward Moultrie.

I called his contact the next week, and we set up an interview. Because I didn't have an audition tape, I read for the general manager, and within a week I received a call offering me a job as a traffic reporter in Atlanta.

5

So I was filled with a huge debt of appreciation to John Freeman for my opportunity, but my mother had been my true rock throughout my life.

For years I had seen her work tirelessly, both in Philadelphia and in Moultrie, but I didn't realize just how much it had taken for her to pay for my education and to keep a roof over our heads. And now that I knew, I missed her even more.

Back home in Philadelphia, my mother had been a maid to one of the city's most respected, highbrow black families. She told me when I was a teenager that she hadn't known what to expect from Eliza Harrison when she first met her. She had thought that she'd be warm like her husband, Louis, whom she had met at Miss Mamie's restaurant on her first day in Philadelphia. Instead, Momma said, Eliza Harrison had been an ice princess.

Sudie, the Harrisons' aging housekeeper, opened the front door when my mother rang the day after she met Louis. From the way my mother told it, she could have been guarding the White House. The Secret Service had nothing on her.

"Good day," Sudie began. She stopped then, taking in the plain brown woman whose demeanor didn't match the stylish black knit dress beneath the black mohair peacoat, a shocking yet fresh design of her own creation.

"How may I help you?" she asked icily.

"I'm here to see Miz Harrison."

"And you are?" the woman questioned. My mother said that if Sudie had worn glasses, that would have been the point at which she would have slid them down her nose and peered over the top of them.

"I'm Georgia Fryar."

"And you're here to see *Mrs.* Harrison regarding . . . ?"

"I'm here to report for work," Momma replied, undeterred by the woman's coolness.

"Oh, you're the one," Sudie said, giving my mother another sweeping glance before stepping aside to let her in.

Momma remembered being enchanted by the crystal turtles that adorned the end tables in the living room, where she stood waiting for Mrs. Harrison. The furnishings were elegant and reeked of wealth. Silver candlesticks holding white candles dotted the room, which was permeated by the aroma of white roses in crystal vases.

A silver frame sitting on the mantel held a photograph of young girls in white gowns and long white gloves. The girls beamed as they stood facing each other, forming a V. A younger, proud-looking Mr. Harrison stood behind one of the girls. My mother noted how handsome and distinguished he looked in his tuxedo. Then she shifted her eyes to the woman standing behind the other girl.

Even in a black-and-white photograph, Mrs. Harrison was radiant. Her hair was piled high, with a few loose tendrils cascading around her shoulders. Her throat was bedecked with jewels that plunged toward her cleavage, which ballooned out over the top of her gown. Her smile was knowing, her stance assured. She was the grande dame, and she knew it.

"That was five years ago at the Gamma Omega Chapter's Debutante Ball."

My mother's head grew foggy as she looked at the angel-faced woman standing before her, whose mouth snapped out words like a slingshot.

"Those are my daughters, Elizabeth and Louise. They're twins. I'm Eliza Harrison. Louis told me that you'd be here at two. It's two-ten. You're late."

"There was a bad accident on Broad Street, and the police wouldn't let anyone through, so I had to walk to 64th Avenue, ma'am."

"Plan better next time, Georgia."

"Yes, ma'am. You have a lovely family."

"Yes, thank you. I'll have Sudie show you around, and I'll meet you back in here shortly."

"Okay, ma'am."

"Good enough."

My mother told me that as she toured the palatial home with its high ceilings and crown moldings, one thought ran through her head. That was "Go on, blacks." Little did she know that, though she embraced them for their prosperity and success, they were indifferent to her, for she was one of "them"—those embarrassing, uneducated southerners who were too stupid to shed the vestiges of their impoverished upbringing.

Momma's life was framed by the Harrisons' whims. She operated according to their meeting schedules, party plans, and vacations, and just as her life revolved around them, my thoughts were trained to center on them as well.

Over time, Momma would come to reveal some of what Louis Harrison had told her about his wife, Eliza, who was black Philadelphia's equivalent of a socialite. The daughter of a prosperous merchant who was also a devoted deacon, and the granddaughter of a teacher who had graduated from Ashmun Institute, now Lincoln University, her familial roots were as straight as the tresses she attended to for thirty minutes every morning.

"Louis, how do you intend to provide for our daughter?" Deacon Pace had asked Louis Harrison.

"Sir, I reckon . . . ," Louis had begun, his own Georgia roots liable to rise to the surface every now and then.

"You what?"

"Uh, I currently work as an apprentice at a mortician's in South Philadelphia, and I plan to open my own establishment within a year, sir."

"I see," Deacon Pace had said, pausing to reflect. "Louis, look at that beautiful flower." He gestured toward the photograph on the desk in his study.

"Eliza is the only daughter I have. Her mother is nearly white, and her constitution is frail. Eliza is the only daughter that the earth did not swallow, and she is precious to us. To me. She has a place in this world, in society. That place is not on the arm of an apprentice. Do you understand what I'm saying to you?"

"I'm not sure sir," Louis had responded, wondering if he

was being politely eliminated from pursuing Eliza's heart and hand.

"Well, let me make it plain for you, son. Before I give my consent to any of my daughter's suitors, for surely you know that you are not the only one, I need to make certain that he can sustain her in the manner to which she is accustomed. The wages of an apprentice will not suffice. I paid for her to attend Cheyney Teacher's College, but my daughter's hands have not known labor, nor will they ever except by her choosing. For that reason, I'm prepared to make you an offer. Because I like you, I'm prepared to give you the sum you need to open your own funeral home. How does that sound to you, Louis?"

Mr. Harrison had paused momentarily, considering what was being offered. He didn't want to start his marriage to Eliza indebted to anyone, most of all her father, for he knew that even with all of the literal wealth that he would acquire, he could never figuratively pay back the initial loan made by a man who believed that every man should make his own way. So without further hesitation, he had said, "Sir, I thank you for the offer, but I respectfully decline."

"Smart answer, Louis. A man always makes his own way, and he certainly never leans on his wife or her relatives for aid. You're a wise young man."

"Thank you, sir."

"So what are your intentions?"

"Mr. Pace, I'll be back here six months to the day to ask for your daughter's hand again. I'll be ready to make her a home that's worthy of her then."

"That's what I like to hear. Six months it is. I'll try to keep the others at bay until then."

"I'd appreciate that, sir."

"You're welcome, young man."

Louis Harrison then set out on a race for Eliza's heart, working full time at the funeral home and in the evening as a janitor at Byberry State Hospital. For the three months before he hung out his shingle, he logged eighty hours a week, fatigue paralyzing him into a comalike sleep from 3 p.m. Saturday afternoon until 8 a.m. on Sunday. Then he would prepare to go to church, where he planted himself two rows behind Eliza and her mother. He was in a race, and Eliza was his prize. And she knew it. That knowledge gave her the confidence to treat him as she desired, according to her whims, for she knew that the dream of her was more than she could ever live up to. But she was determined that he would never know the difference. She was dignity personified. She was elegance epitomized. She was the picture of grace. And so were the daughters she bore him within a year of their union.

Elizabeth and Louise Harrison were just three years older than Momma, but time and circumstance made them as different from my mother as night and day. They picked up where their mother had left off, born with the confidence she acquired from watching Louis slave for her. They behaved the way people do when they know that they are loved, toeing the line between cute boldness and mild disrespect. They had sidestepped formal African American etiquette and dropped the "Miss," calling Sudie by her first name from the moment they could speak. Such insolence from anyone besides Eliza's children would have elicited an evenhanded smack across their twin mouths. Instead, Sudie beamed, gushing, "Ooh, and they speak so clearly."

When Eliza ventured outdoors with them in their stroller with Sudie, the ever-so-dutiful, dark servant, walking two paces behind them, people ogled the two green-eyed, caramel-colored babies.

"What beautiful little angels," ladies would exclaim, feasting their eyes on the youngsters.

"They're going to be heartbreakers," men would profess, clutching their chests dramatically.

Because Louise's hair was jet black and Elizabeth's was auburn, the florist on 5th Street called them Raven and Red. The other shopkeepers, amused by the monikers, took to calling them the same. This habit annoyed Eliza, because she didn't believe in nicknames. In fact, she thought them common. However, because the shopkeepers doted on the girls so much, giving them trinkets and doodads, Eliza granted the indulgence and smiled graciously, enjoying the attention that her children garnered. They were like living, breathing dolls, and she lived vicariously through them.

So after Momma finished touring the home with Sudie, the retiring maid, that first day, she stared at the picture of the four of them, making plans for her own entrée into high society. She had no illusions of marrying rich, for she knew that in this new city she'd never measure up to the refined, native ladies who could have their pick of any monied man. Her chance would come through her sewing needle. And Eliza Harrison had the perfect connections to help Momma get the ball rolling.

My mother had started sewing for her dolls, then for her younger siblings. The older siblings, who were initially reluctant to wear something their younger sister made, soon began asking her to whip something up for them. Their friends began placing orders, and after replenishing her supplies, she saved all of her profits. As a child, her plan had been to move to New York, where she hoped to become a fashion designer. Her parents had said that New York was out of the question, and they told her to think again. When she did, she came up with Philadelphia, the City of Brotherly Love.

Momma generally worked for the Harrisons five days a week, and some weeks the days varied, depending on Eliza's social calendar. Momma worked eight hours a day in opulent East Oak Lane before heading back across Broad Street to the house she rented on Roslyn Street in working class West Oak Lane. There she flipped through magazines that Eliza had discarded, staring at the pictures of socialites in the fashions that wouldn't hit stores for the masses until about a year later. Then she'd sketch the design in her own hand before tracing and cutting a pattern out of newspaper. Her talent was based on intuition.

She had sewn for extra money beginning in sixth grade at the admonition of her mother, who always reminded her five children that they could never go wrong if they took up a trade. My mother, the middle child, was fascinated with fashion, and once in Philadelphia, in no time she found the stores that carried the finest fabrics, which she used on samples to show potential clients once business started trickling in.

Her style icon had been Jacqueline Kennedy, but Momma knew that the woman behind the woman behind the man was actually an African American designer named Ann Lowe. Lowe had designed for American royalty, which included families like the Du Ponts, the Roosevelts, the Vanderbilts, and the Bouviers. She made Jacqueline Kennedy's wedding gown, and was the only African American woman to have a salon in New York's exclusive Saks Fifth Avenue store. Momma admired her work and thought of herself as a fledgling designer, biding her time until she could reach that stature.

She passed a lot of time sketching haute couture designs, waiting for customers to fill in her appointment book and fill out her designs. When she wasn't doing that, she was spending time at Miss Mamie's restaurant, forging a friendship that would evolve into a solid sisterhood over time.

Before I was born, the two of them would sit at the table in the back snapping beans while Miss Mamie began her monologue about what she called the curse of the dark-skinned sister as it pertained to life in Philadelphia. "Take a man like Louis Harrison, for example," Miss Mamie would say.

"Sure, he can waltz in here for lunch daily, fine as a summer breeze on a sultry Georgia day, and he can talk about how good my wrinkled steaks are, and he can stare at my melonlike bosom and apple-round bottom all day, but at night he's gon' return to East Oak Lane and the creamy lady of his dreams.

"And sure, he can bring back trinkets from all of the places he and his wife visit on vacation and deliver them to us, calling us his sensational southern ladies, but women like us can never be the kinds of women who fit the 'high-toned life' that he desires."

When she got to that part, Momma said nothing. She'd just continue snapping beans, sipping on her drink, and only half-listening to Miss Mamie talk. I didn't know it then, but Momma would have a different view of Louis Harrison. It was true that Eliza fit his youthful early dreams and his public life, but she and the materialistic daughters she raised left him wanting something more, something deeper, something real.

Miss Mamie and my mother bantered back and forth for hours, their voices settling into a comfortable, dancelike cadence. Mamie told me later that all the while Claude, the cook, had his eyes on Momma.

I remembered that Mamie usually kept the restaurant open until eight on weeknights, and after she closed, the three of them would sit together sipping the gin that Mamie kept behind the counter. At first Claude would sit quietly, listening to the two women reminisce about life in Georgia. He'd absorb the sound of their voices, whose sweet drawls intensified as they reflected off of each other. When Mamie was the only southerner around, the pattern of her speech sounded lonesome, like a one-shoed walker. But with Momma there, Mamie's walker was complete. And Claude was like the whistle that accompanied the springy step of the walker.

Over time I began to realize that Mamie was a study in contrasts. With her hand on her hatchet beneath the counter, she'd fiercely cuss anyone who looked as if they were about to do devilment in her establishment. Yet her heart was so tender that she'd grow dreamy-eyed as she thought about loves lost, both hers and others'. When she was in those softer moods, it was easy to coax stories out of her. That was how she wove the story of Momma and Claude to me as we sat in my kitchen in Moultrie shortly after my mother died. That was before I'd had the chance to go through Momma's papers and other belongings.

"As the hours passed, Claude would ask your momma to refill his glass. 'Let me have another taste, my ray of sunshine,' he'd say, smiling. And she'd be glad that she was

83

sitting down, because her knees would liquify. Oh, she enjoyed watching him, and she loved talking about him even more. Though he was always jovial, he came alive when he drank. With each drink, his jokes were sharper. He wasn't an aggressive drunk but a funny drunk, and he kept us in stitches when he had a glass in his hand. Your momma said that after all of the despair that had filled her life as the child of Georgia sharecroppers, she knew that she could fall in love with a man who could make her laugh. And that's what she did. *Mm-hmm.*

"Claude would escort your momma home on the nights she came to visit me, riding the subway northbound to West Oak Lane. Then they'd walk slowly up Broad Street to the house she rented on Roslyn Street. As they walked along each took turns talking, delivering soliloquies with heaven-turned eyes gazing dreamily as they spoke. When your momma spoke, Claude drank in her words, almost hypnotized by her speech. He told her once that she could read a grocery list and make it sound divine. She blushed at the compliment, and seeing the reddish hue spread under the brown of her cheeks made him want nothing more than to see her blush like that again. So he delivered compliments to her often, just so he could watch her flush, and just imagine . . .

"Your mother imagined things, too, like how he would look in the mornings entangled in her crisp white sheets as the sunlight crept across his copper skin. She imagined him relaxing under a tree, seeking refuge from the sun that had bent her daddy's back, sipping a glass of lemonade she had squeezed with her own hands. She imagined his lips planting kisses down the back of her neck and along her shoulders. She imagined tracing the mole on his cheek with her tongue. She imagined running her hands across the firmness of his abdomen, fingering the straight hairs on his chest. She imagined that, as his wife, she would bring forth a child whose skin was a cross between his copper and her chocolate. A child whose hair would be a halo of fine brown curls."

With a tear rolling down her cheek, Mamie stopped the story there. She reached out to me with hands whose nails looked like they'd been dipped in blood, and she fingered my curly brown mane. Then she turned her attention to the mound of apples waiting to be peeled and cored.

I knew that I couldn't force her to continue, but I wanted to hear the rest of the story, so I picked up an apple and began to skin it, waiting all the while for her to carry on.

"She was a sweet woman. Reliable, comfortable, and pleasant on the eyes. Built like a typical, corn-fed southern girl. A woman like her would make Claude go out into the world everyday with his shoulders relaxed and his belly full. Without pressure, she'd inspire him to work hard. He'd know that whether he hit the lottery for millions or lost his job, she'd be the same no matter what. She'd welcome him home with a sweet smile, luring him into the kitchen with the aroma of warm biscuits she'd made—from scratch, of course. As he sat at the table a woman like Georgia would drag her hand lazily across his shoulders on her way to the counter, where she was pouring water into the pitcher of iced tea. A woman like Georgia would hum as she stirred sugar into the still-warm tea, shimmying as she worked the wooden ladle around the glass pitcher. And that little shimmy would be all that Claude would need to set him off.

"When they weren't working, they began seeing each

85

other regularly. Your mother started getting a client or two, and she sent part of the extra money that she got from sewing down south to her family. She wanted to get back there for the holidays, but she was counting her pennies, hoping to perhaps rent a storefront by Labor Day, so she promised that she'd get back to Moultrie in the spring. At the time she didn't know that her own momma was ailin', or else she would have gone to see about her. Instead, she stayed in Philadelphia, juggling a Christmas party and two holiday dinners, one for Louis Harrison's side of the family and one for his wife's, since, of course, the two sides didn't get along. The day after Christmas the Harrisons were off to Bimini until New Year's Day. January second was their annual New Year's dinner, and your mother was set to pull together a southern feast to welcome guests for the new year. Until then she was off, and she planned to enjoy herself.

"We all spent Christmas together, and one of my gentleman friends joined us. We were enjoying some bubbly in front of the fireplace when Claude pulled out a box from Baxter's Jewelry. He got down on one knee in front of her and said, 'I know this ain't the traditional southern way, and I haven't asked your father, but I hope that won't stop you from saying yes.'

"I said, 'Fool, you didn't ask the question.'

" 'Sista, hush,' your momma said. Totally shut me up," Mamie said, smiling at the memory.

"Claude picked up then, remembering to ask the question. He said, 'Georgia, would you make me the happiest man in the world by agreeing to be my wife?'

"Child, your mother screamed yes, and she stood up and flung her arms around Claude's neck. I was happier for them than I'd ever been for anybody in my life. So I made the toast.

I'll never forget it. I said, 'The North and South have finally been reunited. May there never be a Mason-Dixon Line to come between your hearts.' It was corny, I know, but we'd been drinkin', so it sounded pretty poetic."

Mamie's hands stopped working, and the pile of dark red apple skins sat like a mountain between us.

"With the Harrisons out of her hair for a few days, Momma spent her mornings at the sewing machine, her afternoons at my restaurant, and her evenings with Claude, planning out the future. They wanted to live in Mt. Airy or Germantown in a deep row house with a large yard and a garage. Their neighbors would know them and their children by name, and the community would feel like an extended family or village. Your mother was positively giddy about the wedding, too.

"They decided on a Valentine's Day wedding. Yes, they knew it was soon, but they figured, why wait? Georgia knew that Claude was the man of her dreams, and Claude knew that Georgia was the woman of his reality, so there was no sense in letting time slip away from them. They were truly in love. Everybody could see it."

A tear rolled down her face, retracing the path of the ones that had fallen earlier.

"But like they say, all good things must come to an end," she said with finality in her voice as she stood up, scooping the apple skins into her apron and walking toward the trash can.

"What happened?" I asked.

"That damn fool! Broke your mother's heart with his foolishness. Everybody in South Philly knew that if you were black, you didn't venture outside after the New Year's Day Parade. Man, those crowds would get so riled up and drunk after seeing the parade that they would carry on hooting and howling like slavery's southern patrollers on a mission. Those damn lawless hooligans would terrorize any lone passerby stupid or slow enough to be caught in the street as the sun fell. We all knew the names of more than a few blacks who had been beaten, maimed, or killed, with no one called to pay for the sins committed on the streets by such a mob. Then there was Claude, tempting fate with a last-minute run over here to get a peach cobbler before heading to your mother's. I told him to either stay here for a few hours or hurry up to the subway station."

Mamie stopped again, angrily wiping at the tears that shocked her with their appearance all these years later.

"He was hardheaded, and he didn't listen. Tol' me to stop worrying and that he would be okay. He was going to meet his Sunshine with this cobbler, and he'd call when he got there. He never called. The police found him the next morning at sunrise in an alley. Beaten to death."

She sighed and sat down again, reaching for my hands.

"And here you are."

So that was the story I believed for years. That Claude was my father. That my mother had been pregnant with me when he had been killed. It was a long time before I learned the truth, and when I did, my heart exploded.

6

Momma had been an incredible seamstress with a true love for fabric, fashion, and the way they came together on the human form. Her clients knew that, and they appreciated the care she gave to each garment, but as her stomach grew, she found it difficult to take on more clients. Her dream of renting a storefront died with Claude, so she contented herself with a small group of customers who called her when they wanted to see new designs. Between her fashion enterprise and her day work, she made a nice living, but in the elite company in which she often found herself working, she saw that money alone was not enough to elevate her status. It was the early seventies, but outside the hippie set, having a child out of wedlock, especially while working for society folks like the Harrisons, did nothing to boost her standing. In fact, it brought her down, and as a child I felt it keenly.

Momma and the Harrison daughters were in varying stages of pregnancy, but Momma felt worlds apart from them because of the differences in their circumstances. After all, Eliza had instructed her daughters to get pregnant as soon as they got married to cement their positions with their new spouses, but Momma's pregnancy was as accidental as they came. Sometimes when Elizabeth Harrison Brooks and Louise Harrison Simpson were over at the house, Momma's discomfort drove her into rooms on the other side of the house so she wouldn't have to face them. But she still saw them, and the sight of them both rubbing their bellies proudly was enough to send Momma to the powder room, where she sobbed quietly beneath the loud sound of the water in the sink running full blast.

Momma rubbed her round belly solemnly, wishing that she had someone to mock-complain about. She wished she could reach out to her own mother to get maternal advice, but she still hadn't told her family that she was expecting. She didn't know how to break such news to parents who had been married for forty-seven years, and who were the products of long marriages that endured despite the harshness of their circumstances. It was one thing for her to call home with a half-hatched dream, but it was something else entirely to call home a broken woman. She thought her voice would betray her, revealing the truth about her shameful state, so she stayed away, virtually severing the ties between herself and her family. Instead, she relied on Miss Mamie and Louis for support.

Louis was like a guardian angel watching over her

throughout her pregnancy. He steered her toward friends who owned furniture stores, where she picked out what she wanted at his expense, and he hired painters, who did impeccable work, to paint the nursery. He was also the one who drove Momma to the hospital when her water broke, and his was the third face I saw through my cloudy eyes. The doctor's was first, and Momma's was second. I counted it as a sign that he had been there to usher me into the world, so I held him in a special place in my heart.

After Momma's six-week maternity leave was over, she put me in a day-care center halfway between our house and the Harrisons'. Although it was convenient enough for her to walk, Louis Harrison drove us home every evening that he wasn't working. I learned to recognize him early, and I'd smile readily when I saw him. I was comfortable with him because he seemed to genuinely care for me and Momma. The two of them talked and laughed easily with each other on the ride home, and their laughter would ascend through the rafters from the kitchen to my bedroom late into the night. It was different from the starched *herr-herrs* they'd offer at the Harrison home. These were belly-busting laughs that would have them doubled over, slapping their knees, with tears squeezing out from the corners of their eyes.

In addition to sharing laughs, Momma and Louis shared meals. These, too, were different from the pretty, tidy meals Momma prepared at the Harrisons' home. These were greasy, smelly, spill-outside-the-lines meals that made them smack their lips, lick their fingers, and sit back in their chairs rubbing their bellies while a chorus of *mm-mm-mm* rose from both of them.

I would come to learn that Momma and Louis Harrison also shared a common history. They both had southern roots, although his weren't as immediate as hers. My mother was born in Georgia. Mr. Harrison's parents had been born there but went north during the first wave of the Great Migration, in the first decade of the new century. According to him, they weren't like a lot of other southern blacks, who shed all vestiges of the South upon setting foot on northern soil. "The Unproud," as his parents called them, changed their sweet, country names and their religious denominations. They purchased hot combs and packed away their colorful speech, exchanging it for the clipped speech that matched the cold air of the North. My mother wasn't like that, and that's what Louis adored about her. Yet for all his veiled adoration of my mother, his wife was the one who bore his name and his wedding band. And that wasn't likely to change.

I caught public transportation to my mother's job every afternoon, and when I got off the bus, I walked to the house and entered through the back door. Just as Mrs. Harrison had told me to.

Over time I began to notice the differences between my mother and Eliza Harrison. I wanted to know what made them so different that a rich, upstanding man like Louis would marry Eliza instead of Momma. And over time I learned that for all my devotion and love for my mother, I didn't want her life. I wanted Eliza Harrison's life, but fear of perceived disloyalty to Momma prevented me from ever admitting that to anyone. So I observed in silence.

The first difference between them was their femininity. Eliza spent hours preening before the mirror to achieve that just-so look she saw in her magazines. Her makeup, flawless. Her hair, held intact with helmetlike precision. Her clothes seemed to be tailored, though she never asked my mother to make one thing for her. Eliza Harrison's high heels clicked on the wooden floors throughout the house, boldly compelling everyone to look, for she was making her entrance. They were in sharp contrast to Momma's plain, rubber-soled "grandma comforts," as I called them, which enabled her to slink unnoticed into any room. Momma didn't have the luxury of tipping around the house bedecked in finery, so she opted for stylishly tailored, well-crafted uniforms. Besides, high heels were too much of a strain, since her girth was steadily increasing. Her petal-soft, wrinkle-free skin was devoid of makeup, and her thick, straight hair, compliments of her Seminole grandmother, was pulled back in a perpetual bun.

Aside from the obvious physical differences, there were atmospheric differences between our homes. In the Harrison home there was always soft music playing. Alternating between jazz and classical, it was always a backdrop, like in a movie. In our house Momma would turn on the radio on Sunday mornings so she could hear the old-time spirituals as they were broadcast on a scratchy AM station. She said that the songs reminded her of her southern home and that music was her only connection to the land she'd left. Other than that, the only other regular sound was that of the sewing machine, which whirred incessantly as Momma fulfilled orders for her clients.

A sound that wasn't heard frequently at the Harrisons' but was enchanting was that of little-girl laughter, which came from Elicia and Lindsay, Elizabeth's and Louise's daughters, who visited a couple of times a week. Their laughter automatically made me smile without even knowing why. Their lives were carefree, and I envied the richness of it because, in my mind, they lived like white girls. Later I would grow to despise their laughter, because it was often directed at me, the bastard daughter of their grandmother's maid. In the meantime, though, it sounded sweet to me.

Another difference between the two homes was the smell. Our house had a stuffiness about it, and it smelled like the heavy processing that permeated the fabric store Momma frequented. On Sundays Momma fried chicken, which we ate for days until Wednesdays, when she fried fish, which carried us through the weekend. In between, I'd catch leftovers from the Harrison home, but in general in our house the smell of oil always hung in the air.

In contrast, the Harrison home was a cacophony of fragrances, but they never overpowered the senses. It was as if each room had its own personality, which was achieved through décor and aroma. The living room smelled of roses, the dining room of jasmine. The scent of cinnamon hung in the air in the powder room, while a pine scent lingered in the study. The aromas continued on the second floor, intensifying in the master bedroom at Eliza Harrison's vanity, where the concentration of sweet scents was intoxicating. That was where Elicia and Lindsay spent a lot of time playing, and on the day they invited me to join them up there, I thought I'd burst from happiness.

The vanity table was shaped like a kidney bean, and it was covered in a sheath of pink silk the color of a newborn's tongue. The matching seat looked like a giant pink pincushion, and the fringe that hung from it reminded me of hair. A pane of glass lay on top of the vanity table. A silver tray with a mirrored base sat on the side of the table. On one was a cluster of jars whose creamy contents were designed to defy time and age. On the other silver tray was a plethora of foundations, mascaras, eye shadows, and tubes of lipsticks in colors ranging from Scarlet to Serenity. Across the back of the table, below the silver-framed mirror, perfumes in bottles too beautiful to think of discarding were arrayed. Their names—Jouissance, Remember, Ascension, Temptation, After—enchanted me. They must have enchanted Elicia and Lindsay, too, for they reached across the ocean of pink silk and grabbed their favorite bottles.

"Go ahead, Claudia, pick one," Elicia said before spraying herself with one of the fragrances.

"Ooo, I love this one," Lindsay commented before squirting her throat with another aroma.

Momma had told me never to play with Eliza Harrison's things, so it was that admonition that echoed in my head. Before I reached for Temptation.

I hadn't recognized the differences in the types of bottles, but when I pulled off the lid, I saw that it was actually a stopper. In my small, seven-year-old hands, the bottle shook, and some of its contents splashed out, landing on my shirt and running down my hand and arm before dripping onto the pink silk of the seat.

"Oh, no," Lindsay cried accusingly. "Look at what you've done!"

"Grandmother is going to be so angry," Elicia echoed, absently reaching toward the table where she meant to place her bottle. Only she missed, and the bottle crashed to the floor.

"Elicia!" Lindsay exclaimed.

"Girls," Eliza called up the stairs, "is everything alright?"

The silence that met her made her rush up the stairs, heels clicking furiously. I recognized the slower, quiet swishing that followed as the sound of my mother in her servant shoes. When they arrived in the bedroom, there we stood,

Lindsay with a full bottle of perfume, Elicia empty-handed, and me, holding half a bottle of evidence. Shattered glass lay on the floor, and an amber puddle lapped at the hem of the pink silk of the vanity stool. From the horrified expression on Eliza's face, it was easy to see what she saw. Lindsay was an innocent. Elicia, whose legs had been pricked by flying shards of glass and who was just now conveniently crying, was a victim. I, the maid's daughter, with my half bottle of evidence, was the culprit. Eliza's eyes burned holes in me as she swooped in and scooped up the barely bleeding Elicia and took her to the bathroom to inspect for imbedded glass. Momma rushed off to retrieve the broom and dustpan from downstairs before returning to clean up the scattered mess. Lindsay had the good fortune to disappear through the rest of the incident, but I bore the shame of watching Momma on her hands and knees cleaning up the mess that she hadn't created. I began to squat next to her in a feeble attempt to help, but the hissing sound she made told me that my help was unneeded. Then I heard the clicking of Eliza's heels as she entered the bedroom again. She looked at the growing stain of the seeping perfume on her delicate pink silk, and she clucked her tongue.

"Georgia, I don't know how you're going to get that stain out of the vanity stool," she said coolly.

"It's okay, ma'am. I'll take care of it."

"Fine," Eliza said, eyeing us wickedly once more before leaving.

The shame I felt that afternoon as I listened to Eliza Harrison rambling on the telephone about how "they-don't-know-how-to-take-care-of-anything-you-can-tell-by-the-way-they-keep-their-neighborhood-and-God-only-knows-how-they-can-stand-to-live-in-those-ratholes-anyway" was overshadowed by the shame I felt later as I watched my mother in the Harrisons' basement misusing her sewing talent by slaving for hours to replace the silk of the pincushion seat where Eliza was going to absently plop her ass. On that day the seed of hatred toward Eliza and all the Eliza Harrisons of the world was planted in me. Other assaults would come over time, and I would grow protective of my mother, who was too tough to need my protection. Nonetheless, I knew that I would never be rid of those elitist snobs who lived lavish, enviable lives, so I decided to do the next best thing: create a lavish, enviable life of my own in any way that I could.

7

Philadelphia is a city of graduated contrasts, and it hasn't changed much since W. E. B. Du Bois penned *The Philadelphia Negro.* The lines between those who have and those who don't, while very real, can be smudged, so it's possible to see a schoolteacher shopping at Saks Fifth Avenue on City Line. Just like it's possible to see a millionaire's son living in a carriage house in the heart of a North Philadelphia slum.

I made no bones about which side of the line I wanted to live on, and gentrification be damned, I wasn't slumming. The closest I came to it was when I visited some of the poor-neighborhood high schools for my mentoring sessions with teenaged girls. It was a project that I'd started in D.C., and I continued it in Philly as a public service through the television station, although whenever I left one of the roach-infested, dingy-looking high schools, I felt the need to go home and shower off the stench of poverty.

The first time I lived in Philadelphia, long ago, before Momma and I left for Moultrie, we lived in a working-class community that was on the downward spiral. Although it wasn't far from opulent East Oak Lane, I felt that I was living on the fringe of life, and I vowed that I'd never do that again. So when I returned, I leased an apartment on the edge of East Falls, a neighborhood on the moneyed side of Germantown, near West Mount Airy, the enclave of wealth populated by the movers and shakers whose jobs require them to live in the city. My apartment was in Alden Park, a complex of three brick-and-pink-marble towers nestled in the woods of Fairmount Park. They boast a view of the city and are within walking distance of the exercise paths that run along scenic Lincoln Drive.

The neighborhood was quaint, but I didn't spend much time exploring it, because I spent my time pouring myself into work. My hours were packed, beginning with a 2 a.m. workout in Alden Park's fitness center. I left for work at three-thirty and was on the air at five. The morning news lasted until seven, and I was back on at nine for *Around Philly*. Then I got another two-hour respite before the midday news, but I often had meetings during that time. After work I researched topics to pitch to my producer, and my legwork was really paying off. I was constantly being recognized by viewers, and our ratings were through the roof.

"Peach, you've got such great ideas. Don't think that the big guy hasn't noticed," my producer commented one day, referring to the general manager. "The big guy" himself had actually complimented me recently on one of my pieces, about a Philadelphia athlete who continued training for the Olympics even after losing both of her parents in a house fire. She had lost everything but the clothes on her back, so I had established a fund for her at a local bank, and it had raised $8,000 in the first two days.

In addition to doing human-interest stories like that, I also interviewed musicians, filmmakers, and authors who came to town to promote their newest works. I had subscriptions to a number of trade publications, and I constantly scanned them to get a heads-up on upcoming movies and books that sounded interesting. I also perused community weeklies on a regular basis. That's what I was doing one afternoon when I stumbled across a familiar name.

ISHMAEL AND ISAAC TAYLOR FIGHT TO RECLAIM CAMDEN, the headline read. My eyes widened with surprise. Ishmael Taylor, my crush from Moultrie State, was doing exactly what he said he'd do all those years ago in his scholarship interview with John Freeman.

"They've done it," I thought in awe as I began to read the article. The reporter almost gushed over the power of their story, outlining Isaac's difficulties and praising Ishmael's strength and how their backgrounds helped to make them effective educators and advocates for change in Camden, New Jersey. According to the article, they were planning a silent auction to benefit Camden Academy, the private boys' school they had founded.

"This is it," I said aloud. "This is going to be my formal introduction to Ishmael Taylor." I reread the article, gleaning details about the event, including contact information for the school, and I immediately placed a call.

"This is Peach Harrison from KPH Channel Six in Philadelphia. How are you?"

"Oh, fine!" the receptionist responded enthusiastically, probably because she recognized my name.

"I understand that a benefit is in the works for the Camden Academy."

"Yes, ma'am. It's scheduled for June nineteenth at seven. It's going to be at the Camden Aquarium, and tickets are $75."

"Thanks for the details. I wonder if Mr. Ishmael Taylor is available to speak with me about publicizing the event."

"I'll check. Hold please, Ms. Harrison."

My heart fluttered as I sat with my ear pressed to the phone. I'd been waiting for this moment for years, and I hoped that my brain wouldn't race ahead of my mouth, making me speak too quickly.

Before another thought could pass through my mind, a man's voice spoke.

"Ishmael Taylor."

"Mr. Taylor, this is Peach Harrison from KPH Channel Six in Philadelphia."

"Hi," he said with a chuckle in his voice. "How are you?"

"I'm great. What's so funny?"

"I just finished watching you on the midday news about twenty minutes ago, and here you are."

"In the flesh," I said, smiling, glad to know that he was a viewer. "I just read about a benefit that you're staging for Camden Academy in a few weeks, and I thought that some publicity could help."

"It certainly could."

"Great. I'd like to bring you and your brother in for *Around Philly*."

"That sounds great. When are you talking about?"

"As soon as possible to help with ticket sales. How's next Tuesday?"

"I'm checking my calendar now, and the morning is open. I need to check with Isaac, though. Can I give you a call back?"

"Certainly," I said before giving him my home business line. "I don't usually do this, but I'm on my way out of the station. Of course, you'll see that the number doesn't get around."

"Of course."

"Okay. I'll look forward to your call," I said. He didn't know how much I meant it.

"Okay. Talk to you soon."

I hung up the phone, feeling like I was floating. It had been a long time coming, but I was finally going to meet the man of my dreams. The man I had first seen years ago at Moultrie State when we were both students. The man whose vision and hard work had catapulted him and his brother out of turmoil and into triumph. The man who I thought would protect and take care of me the way he had done for his brother. The man I had been saving my heart for all these years.

I collected my things and headed out the door, thinking back to the first time I laid eyes on Ishmael Taylor.

I was waiting in the reception area of John Freeman's office. He was planning to come over later that evening, but I wanted to stop by to tell him that I had a study group, so we'd have to meet the next night instead. From outside the door, I heard John's and two other men's voices mingle from behind the cracked door. Checking the day planner on his receptionist's desk, I saw that he was meeting with the finalists for the President's Continuing Education Scholarship. Moving around the reception area, I was quiet as I listened to the conversation coming from his office.

"Philly was right across the bridge, and when we were little, our mom would take us across on the PATCO train. We used to walk around the historic district, visiting the Liberty Bell and the Betsy Ross House and all these other places in Olde City. We didn't have money for the tourist restaurants in that area, so she would buy both of us a soft pretzel and a hot dog and—"

A second voice interrupted, "Yeah, he would gobble up his, and then try to get mine."

"I'm the big brother," the first voice responded.

"Yeah, by three minutes," said the second voice.

All three men laughed loudly before the first voice continued.

"So when our mom would take us to Philly, she'd show us all these historic sites that were important to us as Americans and African Americans. So we learned about former slave and abolitionist Richard Allen and wealthy merchant James Forten. These impromptu history lessons sparked something in both me and Isaac. It stayed lit when we returned home to Camden."

"Ishmael kept his light burning brightly, but mine was dimmed for a little while," the second voice offered. "When our mom got caught up in drugs, we were about to start high school. She didn't have any brothers or sisters, so we got separated and put into different foster homes. My foster mom was just about the check, and her house was in a worse neighborhood than ours was. She didn't care what

I was doing or when I came home, so I just started hanging on the block. It was innocent at first, but then I started hustling. I sold marijuana first, but then moved on to crack. I couldn't see that what I was doing was contributing to the plight of people like our mom. That's why I carry so much guilt now."

Ishmael's voice, the stronger one, chimed in when his brother's faded out. "My foster parents were good. They showed me what hope and hard work could yield. They had always wanted kids, but they couldn't have them, so they treated me like a gift. I tried keeping in touch with Isaac, but after a while, because we went to different schools, and his foster mother never kept a phone bill paid, and the fact that we didn't live near each other, I could barely catch up to him. Junior year, I found out that he was being left back, and he wasn't on schedule to graduate with me. That hurt, because I knew how smart he was, but he was just hurting himself because he had forgotten about the light in himself. During senior year, my foster parents had me filling out college applications, but I knew that I wasn't going anywhere without my brother, so I deferred my acceptances for a year, and I got a job as a janitor at Camden High, where Isaac was going."

"I was shocked the first time I saw him in my school," Isaac said. "But I felt good, because I knew what he was doing. He was waiting for me. And I couldn't keep doing what I had been doing with my big brother there. He wouldn't allow it. And, Dr. Freeman, he was not shy about popping me upside the head for actin' up, no matter who was around. So I had to straighten up, because I got tired of gettin' hit in the head."

They chuckled before Ishmael continued: "My foster parents paid for both of us to come here. They had only budgeted for one student—me—per year, but now they're trying to take care of both of our tuitions, and it's been hard for them. We've both worked at night to help contribute to our education. We're both tired and broke, so that's why we need this scholarship for graduate school. It's hard to keep up this pace and be everything that we need to be for the kids in our community."

John finally spoke: "Both of you have declared yourselves to be education majors. I don't see you just as classroom teachers, although that's a noble job. What's your goal?"

Ishmael answered: "We've already applied for and been accepted into graduate school. We're both pursuing master's degrees. Mine will be in education administration, and Isaac's will be in business administration. We've already done our student teaching and gotten certification in Pennsylvania and New Jersey. So after grad school we'll go back to Camden to open a private school for boys, because these young brothers are in need. We'd like to have all kinds of activities come out of the academy: mentoring, tutoring, educational trips—"

"Things that would have made a difference in our lives as young black men growing up without a father and with a mother who was just too burdened to cope," Isaac added.

"May I ask where your mother is now?"

"She died right after Isaac's high school graduation. Like she was holdin' on for us to be okay."

Hearing that touched my heart and made my eyes well up with tears, because my own mother hadn't been around for my graduation.

I could hear the smile on John's face as he said, "Well, I'm sure that she'd be happy to know that you'll be okay, because the Continuing Education Scholarship is yours."

Their laughter and clapping filled the room before dignified thanks passed from their lips. "We owe you big time," a voice said.

"I look forward to hearing more from you in the future. That's what you owe to your community," John said.

I recognized the sound of him standing and moving toward the door to usher them out, and I busied myself with a magazine. When they passed through the reception area, they nodded at me, and I returned their greeting. The fraternal twins were very handsome, but to me their spirits were even more beautiful. I immediately knew which one was Ishmael, the strong, protective one.

And I fell for him.

I admired his determination to succeed and his dedication to his brother and their community. He inspired me in a way that both empowered and awed me. I remember thinking that a devoted man like that could ground a woman like me. Make me forget about the world because I'd be too busy loving him. Make me believe in oneness—of community and of the heart.

Before he and his brother disappeared, I had etched his face and voice into my memory to treasure. Camden was just over the Ben Franklin Bridge, which ran right into North Philadelphia, and if I knew anything, I was sure that I'd be hearing more from Ishmael and Isaac Taylor once I made my return to Philadelphia.

And the time was now.

I stood in the kitchen of my spacious apartment, drinking a glass of cranberry juice and thinking of the advice Miss

Mamie gave me when I spoke to her on my cell phone on the way home: "Stay cool. Be available, but not too available. When you meet him face-to-face, make eye contact and be confident but a little coy, too."

Before I finished the glass, the phone rang.

"Good afternoon," I said.

"Ms. Harrison?" a male voice questioned. I recognized it as Ishmael, but following Miss Mamie's instructions, I showed no sign of it.

"Yes."

"Ishmael Taylor."

"That was quick."

"I wanted to get back to you as soon as possible."

"I appreciate that."

"Tuesday morning is open for both of us."

"Oh, that's great. I'll need you to arrive at the studio by eight-fifteen. Park in the lot, and check in with security. Someone will meet you downstairs to take you to the green room."

"Okay. Do you need anything from us like background info?"

He couldn't possibly know that everything I needed to know about him had already been committed to memory. So, I said, "Why don't you fax me your bios and some info about the school?"

"Okay."

I gave him the number of my home fax machine, and I was about to try to think of something else to say when he spoke.

"This is going to seem a little offbeat, and I'll understand if you don't have the time to do it."

"What is it?"

"I don't know how well you know Camden, but I'd like to give you a tour of the city before the show so you can see what we're working with. It might help with the interview," he added, trying to convince me.

"That's not a bad idea. When were you thinking?"

"Does Monday at 6 p.m. work for you?"

"Sure. I'll meet you at the school."

"Great. See you then."

"Bye," I said, hanging up and looking forward to my pseudo date with Ishmael Taylor.

8

The Monday before the interview with Ishmael and Isaac was like taffeta. It was hard and scratchy, offering no comfort or relief. It was tense, like a dress fitting in which you know there are pins hidden in the garment to hold it in place, and one false move will jolt you back into still, statuelike submission. It was the choking turtleneck that your mother made you wear in fifth grade when the weather had just turned mildly brisk and you'd rather still be in your light spring jacket that doubled as your early autumn jacket.

I sat at my vanity that Monday, writing out a deposit slip for the rent checks from my properties. I had long since fired Meridius Elkins's company as my property-management firm, and I'd gone with a smaller company whose president I felt that I could trust. He always provided me with the spreadsheets of income and expenditures, detailed accounts of repairs that needed to be made to my buildings, as well as copies of receipts for purchases he'd made for up-keep of the properties. I insisted that all rent checks come to me, though, because as Oprah said, you should always sign your own checks. I included that to mean always sign your own deposit slips as well. With that formula, it was easy for me to know how much money I had.

When I was finished, I studied my reflection. I was sup-posed to meet Ishmael at the school in two hours, but the nervousness gnawing at my gut seemed to be sending stom-ach acids bubbling upward. Sure, he saw me every day on the news, but that wasn't the real me. I'd hidden the real me for a long time, but I needed to unearth it for Ishmael. I wanted to reach out so that he could get to know and love the real me. The one buried beneath the thick coating of cos-metics applied by the makeup artist. The one that was bar-ricaded behind a network of airwaves and wires and a pane of glass. The one that was still reeling from memories of be-ing a fat little girl with a slight stutter, who was sweet and smart and eager to please. It was that willingness to please that made my childhood so painful.

When I reached school age, I spent my days at Cecilian Academy, a private girls' school in West Mount Airy. It was a great school, with small classes and compassionate teachers who nurtured their pupils, instructing us in the art of refine-ment as well as French, English, science, math, and social stud-ies. I also saw a speech therapist for help with my stuttering.

My class was almost like a family. We remembered each other's birthdays and knew each other's siblings. We knew who had started menstruating first, who was doublehanded when it came to jumping rope. We also knew each other's strengths, which we applauded, while we were protective of each other's weaknesses. My classmates knew that I was smart, and they respected my intelligence. They couldn't ignore my weight, my crooked teeth, or my slight speech impediment, but they didn't dare make fun of it. In fact, most days I forgot about it myself.

Things were different, though, when I left school.

I would sit at the kitchen table doing my homework and eating a snack while Momma finished setting the table in the dining room and tying up those loose ends before we left. At exactly four-thirty every day, Mrs. Harrison would glide into the kitchen and look into the pots, inspecting the contents to see what Momma had prepared for dinner.

She never spoke to me until I spoke first to her.

"G-good afternoon, M-M-Mrs. Harrison," I'd stammer, my anxiety triggering a relatively uncommon stuttering fit.

"Claudette," she'd say smugly, alternating between one of the wrong names that she called me. Claudia, Claudine, Clarisse, it was all the same to her. I was nothing more than a chubby little unimportant being occupying a space at her kitchen table, like the spook who sat by the door. Even though I knew the routine, every day I'd sit like an eager pup, awaiting acknowledgment from my master.

It was bad enough that she treated me with such scornful disdain, but she passed that attitude down to her daughters, Elizabeth and Louise, who, though just three years older than my mother, treated her as if she were a rural, unsophisticated child. They, in turn, tried to instill a sense of superiority in their own daughters. In their preteen innocence, Elicia and Lindsay couldn't remember exactly why they were supposed to dislike me, so sometimes they included me in their games. But other times the sense of arrogant haughtiness would stick, and they would remember the schism between people like them and people like me. Then I was fodder for them. They couldn't help it. They had no choice. Elitism had been blended into their blood.

They mastered the etiquette of the elite long before they reached high school. They learned to scribble on Crane's paper, so it was familiar to them when they began writing thank-you notes. They cut their teeth on silver spoons, and the thought of eating meals with anything else did not occur to them. They learned to differentiate between fish knives, butter knives, bread knives, and steak knives long before other kids were even allowed to pick up knives at the dinner table. They made the transition from formula to crystal baby feeding dish without batting an eye.

But for all their mothers' preening and for all their parents' friends' adoration, the cousins, Elicia and Lindsay, were plain girls who could enter a room causing as much of a stir as a turtle disappearing into a pond. Perhaps it was just the awkwardness of adolescence or the strain of trying to follow torchbearers like their mothers. Whatever it was, they paled in comparison to others. While Elizabeth and Louise sauntered into a room, their daughters slunk. Yet people still treated the cousins like princesses. While clothing adorned the voluptuous shapes of the mothers, fabric simply hung on the seemingly lifeless frames of the girls. Yet people still ogled them in their vestments like they were glamorous queens of the catwalk. While their mothers enchanted, or sickened, crowds with their sparkling little stories, in public, Elicia and Lindsay squeezed out words to others when necessary. Yet people still listened to their words as if they were prizewinning orators. They were being trained for a certain place in life. They were being taught that they and their families were the integral creamy center in the dessert of life.

This elitism even crept into the way they worshipped.

Elizabeth and Louise attended St. Luke's Episcopal Church with their families. The fact that Thomas Brooks, Elizabeth's husband, had been raised in the Presbyterian church all his life had not mattered to her at all. St. Luke's was the only place for an attorney of his stature and a woman of her pedigree. So she ignored his protests, and he swallowed a growing pill of resentment, acquiescing to what she insisted was the "right" thing. And every Sunday, Thomas, Elizabeth, Elicia, and Thomas Junior, or TJ, as he was called, strolled into church just late enough to be noticed and sidled into the pew right behind Louis and Eliza Harrison.

Louise, on the other hand, had not had to coerce Gareth Simpson into converting, since he had grown up attending an Episcopal church in his hometown of Richmond, Virginia. He was a third-generation dentist, so he knew the ways of that set. For him, the transition to St. Luke's was made with ease.

Momma and I attended the same church, but for different reasons. She said that she enjoyed the dignified service, and many potential clients were drawn from that lot. But there was another reason we were there. She didn't think that I noticed it, but every now and then I would see her look across the aisle at Louis Harrison. And when Mrs. Harrison was turned in another direction, he would look back.

While Momma was strictly a Sunday-morning member, Elizabeth and Louise joined the appropriate committees, which were the Scholarship Committee, the Women's Committee, and the Community Outreach Committee. In celebration of Women's Emphasis Month, the Women's Committee organized an annual pageant, which was held on the first Saturday in March. The purpose was to showcase the talents of the young ladies in the congregation; the mothers regarded it as an opportunity to show off their daughters.

Elizabeth and Louise were eager to do the same, dull though their daughters were. When the sign-in sheet began circulating, the mothers couldn't sign up quickly enough. Most of the daughters were indifferent to the hullabaloo, but they dutifully accepted their places in the spotlight to be show horses for a day. Stacia Brown, daughter of the city's first black evening-news anchor and her banker husband, would play the harp. Natalie Fields, the daughter of the couple who owned the prosperous supermarket, would do an acrobatics routine. Victoria Ruffin, the daughter of Judge and Mrs. Ruffin, would play the bells. Jessica Upland, daughter of the general manager of the sophisticated set's favorite radio station, would sing a piece from *Evita.* Lauren Merriweather, daughter of the Buick dealer, would play the piano. Elicia Brooks, daughter of Attorney and Mrs. Thomas Brooks, would perform a monologue from *Dreamgirls.* Lindsay Simpson, daughter of Dr. and Mrs. Gareth Simpson, would perform a pointe routine from *Firebird.*

The notion that I couldn't participate never occurred to me. Sure, I had a slight case of stuttering and I was a little pudgier than other kids, but I was bright and personable, and I would make my way through it well. Momma smiled encouragingly when I told her that I'd like to do it, so after church one Sunday she marched over to the sign-in sheet that hung on the wall of the community room and signed me up. I, Claudia Fryar, daughter of domestic worker Georgia Fryar, would recite a poem.

In preparation for the pageant, Momma agonized over the seams of my robin's-egg blue gaucho suit. She toyed with the notion of adding white piping around the collar, but at the last minute she decided not to, opting instead to stay with simplicity. She selected intricately woven knee socks and black patent leather shoes with a heel that, though slight, made me feel mature for my twelve years.

She unwound my thick, wavy hair from its usual bun at the nape of my neck, so my mane billowed around me like a sandy halo. She dotted my lips with a pale rose lipstick, ordering me to blot before adding Vaseline for shine. On my cheeks she dabbed reddish lipstick and smoothed it over where my cheekbones were buried beneath my chubby cheeks. She applied a light dusting of pale blue eye shadow to my lids. With promises of skinning me alive if I so much as lost the back of one, she let me borrow the pearl earrings Mr. Harrison had brought her from Bimini. Only when she was done did she allow me to behold my image in the mirror. I looked beautiful and felt almost carefree, like Elicia and Lindsay. I felt like a princess, and I had hopes of ruling the realm that Saturday afternoon. But I was still nervous.

I rehearsed my lines in my head on the bus ride to the church, and with every stanza firmly etched into my memory I felt ready.

"Speak clear, now," Momma admonished, shifting her feet around the large shopping bag squished between her knees. Discomfort was stamped on her face as she sat squeezed in the narrow seat, spilling over onto me so as not to offend the mass-transit rider on the other side.

"Yes, Mother," I returned brightly to the warning that she hadn't had to give. I was the one who studied Stacia Brown's mother on the TV news every evening. Her words weren't too round, like Momma's, nor were they clipped, like Eliza Harrison's. They were smooth without flowing into each other, distinct without being stiff, clear without being awkward. In my mind I knew how to articulate, and with my exuberance I knew how to make people listen.

When we got off the bus at St. Luke's, I looked up at the sky. The gray haze overhead and the muggy air threatened rain, but I didn't let that dampen my spirits. I was going to do a good job and make Momma proud. When we entered the community room, Louis Harrison, who had been prodded into acting as the master of ceremonies, waved to Momma and me. He gestured toward the table where his wife sat, fanning herself while chatting with another woman.

"Georgia! How lovely to see you," Eliza exclaimed with false enthusiasm.

"Miz Harrison, how do you do?" Momma said, sitting down.

"Grand. Just grand," she replied, dabbing at the moisture gathering on her forehead and top lip. "If these personal summers of menopause would slow down, I'd be even better," she confided, leaning in closer to my mother as if they were good friends.

I knew that she hardly uttered two cordial sentences to my mother during a normal day, and now she was cozying up to her, attempting to demonstrate how liberal-minded she was to talk with her help in a social environment. I almost sucked my teeth, thinking of what a phony she was.

Eliza Harrison's eyes snapped in my direction. "You look lovely, dear."

"Thank you, Mrs. Harrison. As do you," I replied, syrup oozing from each word.

"Georgia, you should be so proud," she marveled, looking from me to my mother.

"I sure am," Momma replied confidently, picking up the program booklet that had been left on the chair.

I breathed deeply, looking at the program over Momma's shoulder. I knew that she wanted me to do well, but I didn't know just how much my performance mattered to her until I felt her hand shaking as she clutched my fingers.

"Excuse me," I said, scooting out of my chair and beckoning her to follow me to the ladies' room.

She moved slowly, her portly frame hindering her speed.

In the bathroom, she gazed at me in the mirror while she adjusted my collar for what seemed like the tenth time. She mumbled, "I shoulda put that pipin' on here like I thought to."

"Mother, stop," I said calmly, taking her hand. "It's very pretty the way it is."

She blinked hard, swiping at her eyes before speaking. "Claudia . . . ," she began.

With words stuck in her throat, she couldn't continue, but her trembling conveyed all of her hopes and wishes to me.

"You better than me," she whispered, with a tear making a path down her sweet plump face. "You better than me," she repeated, pulling me toward her and enveloping me in her warm embrace. I felt the slight quaking of her flesh as she cried, murmuring gentle words.

"I know ain't none of this been easy for you. Having only me, and having to live up under people like them, but, baby, just like you better than me, you better than them. And you gonna show 'em. Today and forever. You gonna show 'em, baby. You hear?"

"Yes, Momma," I said, my face still pressed against her heart.

"Say Mother. Always call me Mother, but think of me as your lovin' Momma," she corrected.

I nodded my understanding. She didn't want me to sound like her. She wanted me to be better.

"Alright now." She pulled away from me, double-checking my makeup to see if she had smudged it. I didn't care if she had. She was my Momma, and I loved her.

"Now do good, girl," she said, smiling. She took my hand, and together we exited the ladies' room, heading back to the table and settling in to listen to the three young ladies who would take center stage before I did.

"W-w-womanhood is . . . ," my voice rang out clearly.

"Womanhood is finesse and fire, both emotions mingling in one soul. / Womanhood is politeness and power, both holding equal importance. / Womanhood is fighting with the heart and the head, enjoying the thrill of the intellectual hunt while also knowing when to embrace. / Womanhood is sensitivity and strength . . . uhm . . . the two fulfilling at once the needs like yin and yang. / W-w-womanhood is dignity and devotion, keeping your head up while keeping your nose to the grindstone. / Womanhood is . . . uhm . . . compassion and courage, because compassion is what moves us to act and courage is what keeps us . . . uhm . . . "

My mind drew a blank, but I improvised with a smile.

". . . c-c-compassion is what moves us to act and courage is what keeps us on the stage."

The audience smiled and applauded at my quick recovery.

"Womanhood is grace and gratitude. Both make us humble and help us to remember that we've come thus far with help. / Womanhood is character and confidence. Character is the constant even when . . . uhm . . . confidence is elusive. / Womanhood is you today, and womanhood is us tomorrow."

I paused before stepping back from the microphone and taking a deep breath. The audience burst into applause, and I bowed my head slightly before making a slight curtsey.

My mother was on her feet, clapping loudly and smiling broadly. None of the other parents had responded so animatedly, but I wasn't embarrassed. I was simply glad that I had made Momma proud. With my head high, I returned to the table, acknowledging the audience with nods and smiles.

Beaming like a proud father, Louis Harrison spoke: "And with that powerful delivery of 'Womanhood Is,' we are now going to enjoy lunch, which has been catered by St. Luke's own Sugar Bryant, owner of Sugar's Shack. Pastor Oreland will come forth and bless the food."

Momma squeezed my hand through the prayer, and once the congregants opened their eyes again, she beamed proudly at me, saying, "You done good, girl." Then she reached down inside the bag she'd been carrying, and she pulled out a bouquet of white roses.

"Thanks, Mother," I returned, kissing her on the cheek. The kiss sent tears down her cheeks, and she excused herself.

As the Harrison clan settled in at the table, Louise turned to me. "You did a beautiful job, Claudia. I love that poem."

"Thank you, Mrs. Simpson."

"Yes, dear," Elizabeth chimed in. "You did a fine job, but here's a tip," she said, leaning toward me across the table.

"Watch your 'uhms.' You must have said it ten times, and it was getting a little distracting."

The smile fell from my mouth.

"Elizabeth," her husband snapped. "The child did fine."

"I was just giving the girl a helpful hint," she said through clenched teeth.

"Claudia is much more articulate than I was at that age," Louise commented, trying to smooth the waters and make people forget what a bitch her sister was.

But I didn't forget.

"Great job, young lady," Louis Harrison said, approaching the table with Pastor Oreland in tow.

"I think I'd better watch my back, or she'll have my job," the pastor said, patting me on the shoulder reassuringly.

I chuckled, happy for the diversion from the tension that had permeated the air just moments before. I heard Pastor Oreland blathering, pouring compliments on a family that needed no ego boosting.

". . . always so lovely. Even when they were babies, they were breathtaking. Now they've got little ones of their own, who are equally dazzling," the pastor lied, grinning stupidly at Elicia and Lindsay. "And handsome, too," he added, patting Thomas Junior on the shoulder.

After a lunch of crab-and-Brie soup, spinach salad, chicken remoulade, Parmesan mashed potatoes, and sweet-potato cheesecake, the other participants moved backstage to ready themselves for their performances.

Elicia was the first to take the stage, after her grandfather introduced her.

And she fumbled royally, unable to will the words to come out and incapable of muttering anything intelligible.

Elizabeth's head went down, and she fought the urge to sink into her seat. Meanwhile, her husband looked sympathetically at his daughter as she struggled onstage. He rose to meet her near the bathroom, where he knew she'd rush as soon as she unglued her feet from the stage. Elizabeth rose as well, but she walked outside to the parking lot, where she slumped into her Jaguar, pulled out a cigarette, and inhaled deeply.

After the rest of the performances, Louis returned to the podium, where he thanked the participants and their parents. He warned everyone to stay dry, since the sky had opened during the time we were inside. He smiled and left the podium, making the rounds and saying his good-byes before going to collect his wife.

Momma said, "If it's raining, there's no sense in venturing down to Mamie's. Let me call her to let her know that we'll come tomorrow."

She fished some change out of her purse and made her way to the pay phone by the ladies' room. I stood, staring at my roses and nodding at the well-wishers who passed by on their way out to the parking lot.

By the time Momma returned, the community room was almost empty, and we made our way outside. A bus was easing away from the curb just as we approached, and Momma thought that she could get the driver's attention.

"Wait," she yelled as she pushed her body into action, not even bothering to open the umbrella. She began running, dragging the paper bag, which grew more and more tattered as the fat drops of rain crashed against it.

"Hol' it. Hol' it now. Wait!" she whooped, her screams unheard by the bus driver.

I ran behind her, my patent leather shoes sloshing through puddles the size of ponds. "Stop!" I yelled. But the bus driver didn't hear me either.

Drenched and winded, we settled beneath the arch that city officials had built for those who rode mass transit. My white roses had lost most of their petals in the scramble and my hair, having frizzed from the earlier humidity, was now a thick, soggy mass that lay on my shoulders.

Disappointed, Momma breathed heavily, attempting to wipe her face with a napkin from her pocket. With her head buried in the thin napkin, Momma didn't see the car. But I did.

And the passenger, Eliza Harrison, saw us. And as she passed by, with Louis in the driver's seat and the backseat empty, I saw her smile before turning away.

I fought tears of remembrance from soaking my cheeks as I brushed powder onto my face, readying myself for my meeting with Ishmael. I tried to smile, imitating my on-air confidence, but the smile looked fake.

"Who can love a stuttering little fat girl?" I asked, remembering my old self before letting my head fall and giving in to the tears.

9

I once heard Donna Karan say that a woman's shoulders are the last thing to go as she ages. With that in mind, I donned a peach-colored silk Donna Karan wrap dress that revealed a hint of cleavage, the illusion of leg, and a taste of shoulder as it skimmed my curves. Miss Mamie would have been proud. I had washed my hair and let it dry into naturally loose curls that just dusted my shoulders. Large gold hoops and a few thin bangles added a simple yet artistic flair to my ensemble while gold Greek goddess–inspired sandals screamed of sex appeal.

I arrived at the school at exactly 6 p.m., bearing small tokens for Ishmael and Isaac. In a gold gift bag I carried two peach rose boutonnieres for them to wear on the show. I marched up the path toward the large Victorian building they'd purchased for use as a school. An annex had been added at the back, and a huge yard was filled with neatly cut grass, benches, and shade trees. The brothers met me on the steps of the school, and Ishmael waved as I approached.

Although they were twins, their resemblance ended with their birthday. Isaac, who was thin, slight almost, was the color of dry playground dirt, with no distinguishing features except a latent sense of edge that had been cultivated on the corners of Camden's mean streets. Ishmael, on the other hand, was golden, with dark brown curly hair framing his face. A goatee that would look cheap on another man called attention to two fleshy lips that I wanted to suck. His slim build, though hidden under a cobalt blue suit, was packed with lean muscles, and I yearned to be within his arms. Ishmael stood with his hands in his pockets, while Isaac's arms were folded across his chest.

"Hi," I said cheerily as I approached them. I turned to Isaac first, nodding hello before extending my hand. "Peach Harrison."

"Isaac Taylor," he responded, offering a slight smile.

I turned my attention toward Ishmael and flashed a smile before saying, "Hello, I'm Peach. It's a pleasure."

He returned the smile, saying, "The pleasure's mine. I catch you on the morning news pretty regularly."

"Oh. I don't really laugh that much off camera," I said, referring to the ebullient persona that I adopt for the morning news.

"No, it's fine. It's refreshing. Morning's my favorite time of day. You and your cohost get me geared up to go."

"That's good to know."

I continued smiling, thinking, "Wow, I hadn't even had to turn on the charm. He was already circling the boat."

Isaac said, "Peach, I'm not going to be able to join you

guys for the tour. I have to meet with one of the board members. You'll be in good hands with Ishmael."

"Okay," I responded, pleasantly surprised. "Before you go, let me give you this to wear on the show tomorrow."

I reached into the gift bag and retrieved one of the containers holding a peach rose.

"Thank you," he said, smiling. "See you tomorrow."

"Bye," I said as he walked off, leaving me with the man of my dreams.

"So this is it, huh?"

"Yup," he said proudly, though obviously tired from a day's work. "Let me show you around." He opened the door and ushered me inside the building, where he proudly pointed out classrooms and offices. Then we went into his office so he could grab his keys, and while he did, I quickly scanned the place, looking for signs of a womanly touch. Seeing none, I relaxed as he ushered me out to the parking lot, where we got into his car. Driving out of the lot, we passed my gold Mercedes.

"Must be yours," he said, smiling.

"Why do you say that?"

"It's elegant, and it looks like something you'd drive."

I smiled at his compliment and settled back into the passenger seat of his sensible sedan.

For the next few hours, Ishmael drove me around Camden, showing me where the brothers had grown up, where Isaac had stayed with his foster mother, and the neighborhood where Isaac had hustled. Then Ishmael took me to the tree-lined streets fronting large single homes where he had stayed after being brought into the foster-care system. Seeing the contrast between the environments stoked a dormant fire within me. All of my experience had taught me that people who had the world delivered to them on silver platters didn't appreciate their birth circumstances, while those born into poverty spent their days cursing their lot. Would I have been an appreciative, hardworking person if I had been born into financial comfort? Or would I have taken my condition for granted like the Harrisons or the students at Moultrie State whose dorms I had cleaned? Would Isaac have been a stronger person if he had been taken into Ishmael's foster home? Would Ishmael have succumbed to the pressures facing impoverished urban males if he hadn't been given that solid support from his foster parents?

It was as if he had read my mind as those thoughts passed through my head.

"I used to feel what some call survivor's guilt when I finished high school and I saw the problems that Isaac was having. I kept asking God, 'Why me? Why was I selected to be in that good home with good foster parents while my twin brother had to tough it out in the rough part of Camden?' It used to eat me up. That's part of the reason I stayed here that extra year. I knew that I didn't want to do anything, be anybody successful, without my brother by my side. Life would be almost corny without him," he said with a laugh.

"Do you still feel the guilt?"

"Sometimes. Like when something comes harder for him. I'm always thinking that it was the training I got from my foster family that makes that obstacle easy or nonexistent for me. And my brother just got dealt a bad hand," he explained, looking into my eyes as we sat at a red light. "It's times like that when I question God," he admitted, seeming ashamed.

"I have questions like that, too," I said, downplaying the anger I often felt at being born into my circumstances, which, while not horrid, had made me into the monster that I felt like.

"I think that the questions make me—us—double-check ourselves. It's people like us who God uses to make big, powerful statements. Like with the work Isaac and I do, we're just trying to right some of the societal wrongs that we see here in the city," he said, gesturing to the world outside his car.

"Camden has so much to offer, but the political leaders have pretty much been opportunists. For example, why would any official agree to have a prison built on his city's waterfront? That's prime development property, and it could be turned into an outdoor theater, a restaurant district, or even condominiums. Then, not more than five miles away, there's another prison, and people stand outside doing sign language with the prisoners. These are folks who society labels as unteachable, yet they pick up sign language, which I don't think is a class that's taught in prison.

"Meanwhile, the schools are in really bad shape, and it's not because the teachers don't want to do their jobs. They're overworked, underpaid, have limited supplies, and they're trying to teach kids, many of whom come to school hungry or high or both. Parents are falling down on the job. They expect the schools to do everything, and the teachers simply can't. That's why we had to lay out some ground rules for parental involvement at our school," he explained.

As he began talking about the school he and Isaac had founded, he beamed with pride, and I hung on his every word, buying into his dream.

"I'm the head of school at Camden Academy, and Isaac

heads development. The school started off pretty small, but every year we add a grade. Now we're up to the sixth grade, and the numbers are steadily growing. We have a board. The members include businessmen, two professional athletes, and a few regular folks, who keep us on our toes. The board members do a good job with steering money and opportunities our way, so we can keep tuition relatively low and achievement pretty high. Our students are all young men, and they wear uniforms. They all have mentors, and we actually build weekly mentoring time into the schedule, because it's really important for them. We have guest speakers, assemblies, and field trips—all the things that have been cut from the budget in public school districts across the country. So basically we're trying to change the world one child at a time."

I let his words sink in before I remarked, "It sounds like a phenomenal place."

"It is. I can truly say that I love my work."

"That's important."

"You sound like you don't enjoy yours," he commented.

"I do, but it sounds so trivial next to yours."

"Not at all. We're both disseminating information. Keeping folks in the know."

"I suppose. I also do a little volunteer work with teenaged girls. I started the program years ago when I was in D.C., but now I just participate every now and then. Other reporters are more active in it than I am. I'm just the figurehead now, but it's still something I enjoy."

"That's good stuff. Community service is a must for community progress," he said, smiling.

I smiled in return, but I said nothing more.

"Tell me more about yourself? Start with the name. Peach obviously isn't your real name."

"No. My real name is Claudia. An old friend gave me the nickname," I said, thinking back to John Freeman.

"Uh-oh. The 'old friend' thing. I'm calling you Claudia, then," he said, laughing.

"Really, it's not all that," I responded, trying to downplay John's role in my life. Truth be told, he was the exact reason that both of us were where we were today, at least in part.

"I really haven't been serious with anyone," I continued.

"Why's that?"

"Work," I replied matter-of-factly.

He laughed. "That's taken up all of my time, too. I don't know too many women who'd willingly accept second place to my job."

"You never know. There just might be someone who'll recognize that you're worth every second of the wait," I replied, touching his hand lightly.

He was quiet for a few seconds before saying, "The woman I settle down with is really going to have to be understanding and know what she's getting into."

Then he looked at me soberly. I smiled at him, staring into his eyes before looking out the window.

The rest of the evening was a dream, and I couldn't believe how everything fell into place. Things never worked out well for me, so I virtually held my breath, afraid that something would shatter the perfection of it all. The chemistry between us was electric, and I knew that he was as drawn to me as I was to him. As I began to relax I was hopeful that finally my life was taking shape the way I'd always hoped it would.

We drove across the Ben Franklin Bridge into Philly and parked near the art museum. Then we climbed the steep steps and perched ourselves at the top to take in the view of the city from on high, where we watched tourist after tourist bound up the steps in their best imitations of Rocky Balboa. Although the museum is closed on Mondays, tourists can't resist seeing the place Sly Stallone made popular on film.

He asked me questions about my childhood, and I was pretty honest with him, though omitting the emotional ugliness that had plagued my life. As for my education, I told him that I, too, had attended Moultrie State but that life had been my great teacher.

One of the things John Freeman used to say was that, next to books and senior citizens, travel was a great educator. Sitting with Ishmael under the stars, I was convinced of it. The traveling I'd done up the East Coast had been good for me, because I was able to talk to Ishmael about some of the things I'd seen, from historic sites and national landmarks in one city to museums and restaurants in another.

Ishmael was taken by me. I could see it in his eyes. But just to intensify his attraction to me, I pulled away, telling him that I was having a great time but I needed to get home to get some sleep. He looked mildly disappointed, but I reminded him that I'd see him in a few short hours at the television station.

"Get a good night's sleep," I said when he pulled in front of the school. "Eight fifteen will be here before you know it. Are you nervous?"

"A little," he admitted.

"Don't worry. You'll be fine. Just tell your story, and you'll inspire us all."

"I like your optimism," he said, pausing awkwardly, obviously not ready for the evening to end.

"Thanks." I touched his hand, reminding him of the lateness of the hour by pointing to the clock on the dashboard, which read eleven thirty.

"I had a good time," I said, leaning over and kissing him on the cheek before putting my hand on the door handle.

"Me, too. Oh, I'll get that," he said, hopping out of his side and walking over to mine. He helped me out and walked me to my car.

"Good night," he said, standing close to me.

Heeding Miss Mamie's advice, I backed away.

"Good night," I said, smiling from the driver's seat.

I started my car and pulled off into the black velvet of the night.

The interview flowed like butter. He and Isaac both wore their peach boutonnieres, and I smiled with recognition when I saw them. Just beneath the professional façade I maintained—because, after all, this was my job—was a layer of flirtation that I exuded and Ishmael could feel.

When we concluded, I hugged them both, telling them what a pleasure it was to have spent time with them. Isaac thanked me again, and he headed off toward the stairs leading out to the parking lot.

"I had a good time talking to you last night," Ishmael said. "I'm running on vapors right now, but I'm going to suffer for the late night later on."

"And the day's just started," I said.

"I know."

"I could stand here talking to you forever, but you'd better go. You don't want to be late getting back to your students."

"Yeah. I can't stand lateness, and I try to drill that into their heads, too."

Looking at him doe-eyed, I asked, "Well, is this good-bye?"

"It doesn't have to be, especially since I'm right across the bridge."

"It would be great to see you again," I ventured.

"I was thinking the same thing. You know, I don't have a date to the auction."

"Oh, yeah?" I responded with a small smile. If he wanted me to go, he'd have to ask me.

But waiting for him to do it was killing me.

"Would you . . ."

"Yes," I practically shouted before he got the question out.

My heart was pounding as I thought about what I wanted to say next. I wanted to tell him that he didn't need an occasion to see me and that I'd be available any time he wanted me, but I was thinking that I didn't want to rush because I wanted a lifetime with him. Words from *Romeo and Juliet* came to mind. I accidentally spoke them aloud: "Wisely and slow; they stumble that run fast."

"What was that?" he said with a queer grin on his face.

"Nothing," I replied, annoyed with myself for speaking my thoughts aloud.

"No, seriously. Repeat it."

" 'Wisely and slow; they stumble that run fast.' That's what Friar Laurence says right after Romeo tells him that he met the woman of his dreams at a party the previous night."

"Oh, yeah?" he inquired, smiling. "Should I take your advice?"

"I wasn't advising."

"Well, what do you think?"

"I don't know what you're asking."

"That's probably because I haven't been clear. Let me make it plain now. It sounds a little strange, though. I just met you last night, but it seems like I've known you for a long time. Kind of like two puzzle pieces that have been floating around without each other, maybe never even knowing that they were supposed to be a match. But when they finally come together, they fit. I feel like a fool saying this, 'cuz I'm from Camden," he teased, thumping his fist on his chest mockingly in a masculine show of strength. "And I wouldn't say it unless I felt something coming from you. So, truthfully, I don't know what I'm asking, Claudia. But I want to know if you hear what I'm saying."

I grabbed him by the hand, leading him away from the open set toward my office. There I sat on my desk and looked him in the eye.

"Ishmael, I hear exactly what you're saying, but I don't feel like a fool admitting it. It was one thing to read your story and feel like you were a kindred spirit. It's another thing to meet you and talk to you for hours, knowing that you are. But it's rushed, and I want a lifetime of love. Do you understand what I'm saying?"

"I think so. I want you to know that I don't have time for games, Claudia Harrison, so when I commit, it means something. If you accept that, I'll kiss you right here and right now."

I nodded my head slowly, accepting his words, his proposition, and his affection. The blood swishing past my ears threatened to deafen me as I looked into the eyes of the man I'd wanted for so long. My lips tingled with hopeful anticipation that I would be his choice, that he wanted me as much as I needed him to want me. I needed his embrace and his love.

So when he moved across what seemed an acre of carpet that separated us, it couldn't have been fast enough. And when his lips met mine, after years of longing for him, lightning struck, and I collapsed in his arms, knowing that my life would never be the same.

I was sitting at my desk, doodling Ishmael's name like a schoolgirl and still floating from his kiss, when my producer, Diana Davis, came in.

"Peach," she said in her usual peppy manner.

I smiled at her enthusiasm. She was always so eager and brimming with new ideas that working with her was a pleasure. Both of us came up hard, she in working-class Fishtown and I in West Oak Lane, so we both had something to prove. I always felt like she was in my corner, pulling for me to be my very best, and I knew she felt that my work was a reflection of her. So we benefited from each other's success.

"What's up, Diana?"

"I've gotten two press kits and five phone calls about this already."

"What?"

"A fiftieth-anniversary conference that will be here in three weeks."

"What's the organization?"

"It's something called The Inner Circle, and apparently it was founded here by some society matrons whose last names are Pennington, Harrison, Walton, and Chambers. Have you ever heard of it?"

Had I? It was an organization that I cherished for the opportunities it provided for African American children but despised because of my exclusion from it. I didn't want to go into that with Diana, though. She wouldn't understand it, because it was a group that was under the radar for most folks unless they were in the loop, so I simply nodded.

"Here's the press release and some accompanying literature. Look it over, and let me know how you feel about devoting a segment of the show to it."

"Okay," I said, trying to quell the uncertainty swirling in my stomach.

"Alright. By the way, I loved that Taylor segment. That Ishmael is a cutie," she said, straightening up and readying herself to leave.

"He sure is." I smiled dreamily, returning momentarily to my happy thoughts of him.

"Uh-oh. I'll leave that alone for now." She grinned.

I smiled at her again before my eyes returned to the press kit before me.

"What am I going to do?" I murmured to myself. I wasn't quite ready to face that society set yet. Since my return, I'd socialized along the fringes of that circle, having garnered invitations to different events, but most of my time had been spent working. After all, success has always been the sweetest revenge, and because I'd been bilked out of hundreds of thousands of dollars, tormented like a leper, and banished from my hometown like a criminal in a cowboy movie, I definitely had an ax to grind. But now my shame-filled past and my successful present were about to collide head-on, and I wasn't sure that I was ready for it.

"Damn," I said as I sank back into my chair in exasperation.

10

It wasn't until I was twenty-one that I was sure of something I'd suspected all my life. Momma and Louis Harrison had been embroiled in a romantic affair for years. From what I gather, it wasn't a series of steamy, passionate interludes in which they planned secret getaways. Nor was it a relationship that Momma secretly took pride in holding over Eliza Harrison's head. It was simply a secret union that was formed after Claude's death, when Momma was heartbroken and the perpetually lonely Louis Harrison stepped in to comfort her. That friendly comfort, born of the seed of similar backgrounds, evolved over time into something that both of them needed and cherished. He could talk to her, unafraid of having his roots show. He could just sit and let the weariness of his busy, shallow life ooze out of him as she massaged his shoulders. He could be the man that he had been raised to be, caring and sensitive, rather than the shell-like image of the man he transformed himself into. The dapper, charismatic man who fit the profile of Talented Tenth success.

For him, Momma was the same as she was for me—steady, secure, comfortable. All the things Eliza wasn't. He said so in his letters, which I found after I buried Momma.

The letters were in a lockbox along with her birth certificate and mine, which actually bore his name. I had never seen mine, and I thought, because my given name was Claudia, that Claude was my father. I'd never known the circumstances or date of his death. I only know that his picture sat on Momma's dresser throughout my childhood, and when I asked her once who it was, she said with a sad sigh, "Claude." I never wanted her to dwell on sadness, having to revisit that pain, so I didn't ask any more. Some nights when I couldn't sleep, though, she'd sit me on her knees and rock me, weaving tales about my father, whom she called a noble man, never referring to him by name. She'd simply begin by saying, "Your father, the noble man . . ."

And then she'd tell a majestic story about his generosity or his kindness. and that would be that.

After finding out the truth, I realized that Momma had had her reasons, the most obvious being Louis Harrison's marital status. But that, of course, meant that I was a Harrison, and I'd been robbed of the benefits and esteem that came with that.

That meant that when Alicia and Lindsay had committed their aversion to me to memory, and had called me a bastard, in actuality they were calling their aunt out of her name.

So when Elizabeth actively and Louise passively through association had looked at me with disdain, pointing out my flaws and mocking my ignorance of some social graces, they were spurning their sister, too.

And that meant that when Eliza "accidentally" locked me in the cold, dark basement for hours after sending my mother out on an errand and sending me down for a bottle of wine, she was turning her back on her husband's illegitimate daughter.

And they knew. They had to. I had his teeth, long and rectangular like Chiclets. Those teeth would have made a pretty smile had they not decided that they needed growing room. Braces, applied after I landed in Moultrie, had been my saving grace. But that hadn't helped me as a kid, when it was one more flaw to point out.

In addition to the teeth, I had Louis's hands—those same bony fingers with knobby knuckles and broad nailbeds curving to hawklike points. In his work, his fingers concealed the scars and wounds of the dead but they had also given life to my mother in the form of the letters she had tied with red ribbons and sprayed with cologne before sealing them in a plastic bag and packing them into the lockbox that sat in the corner of her closet. Sixteen years' worth of letters that validated my existence, chronicled by date and compiled neatly, kept perhaps for me to read one day. Crisp bills were folded into them. Unused, perhaps saved for me. But that would never be enough to make up for the shame and pain of my childhood. Neither could the sweet words that were written in the letters, but at least they were a salve, confirming that my mother, the poor woman who had taken care of everyone else's needs while ignoring her own, had been loved.

Although I was hungry for information about their relationship, I took my time reading Louis's letters. I had to digest them slowly, savoring each nuance, each hint of the events, musings, and feelings he'd shared with her. I found them after graduating from Moultrie State as I was packing my things in preparation for my move to Atlanta and my new life. I hadn't had the heart to go through Momma's things after she'd died; I'd simply closed the doors to her bedroom and sewing rooms and looked away whenever I'd had to pass them. But leaving Moultrie meant bringing closure to more than my education. I had to tie up all my loose ends.

After meeting with my father's attorney just before starting my career in Atlanta, I sat in the bar of my Center City hotel, downing a shot of Grey Goose and thinking about my predicament. It had been a disappointing meeting, and I needed to get another perspective. It was times like this that I sorely missed my mother. I didn't have her, but I went to my room to call Miss Mamie, who was the next best thing.

The advice she gave was sensible, but not quite what I wanted to hear.

"Claudia, you're pressed for time, but if you really want to know what you're missin', chil', go around and see those fourteen properties. Then decide if they're worth pursuing."

"But, Miss Mamie, aren't they all worth pursuing? They're mine."

"Yes, they're yours, but are you up for what surely will be a long, drawn-out fight? You're about to start a new life hundreds of miles away. Do you want to do it with old baggage?"

"Yeah, if that baggage contains money. My money."

She laughed before saying, "Okay. It's just my opinion. Trust yourself, though."

"Okay," I consented before hanging up the phone.

I called the bell stand and asked for my rental car to be brought around. Then I freshened up, grabbed the file, and made my way downstairs and out to go search for my inheritance.

The properties were scattered throughout various parts of the city, and their worth varied accordingly. Seeing some of the more humble-looking buildings made me grateful that my father had thought about my future, but seeing some of the nicer ones fueled my desire to go after Eliza Harrison to exact revenge on her for denying me what was rightfully and legally mine.

By one-thirty in the morning, I'd seen all of them, and as I sat in the car thinking, I vacillated between anger, because I'd lost so much that I never knew I had, and peace, because I still had something. As I sat rubbing my tired eyes, I was determined more than anything to find out why. So I drove to East Oak Lane.

I pulled up in front of the Harrison house, the house that held so many bad memories of my youth. I got out of the car, marched toward the house, and rang the doorbell. When I got no answer, I banged on the glass pane of the storm door. Still, no response. I banged harder and shouted up to the bedroom window.

"Open the door, you coward. I know you're in there. Come on down and face me, you old bitch."

I continued banging until exhaustion forced me to sit down on the front step. Closing my eyes, I leaned against one of the stone lions that flanked the steps, and I reflected on my past. There were times when Eliza would send my mother to the store in search of some trivial item, and while she was gone I'd have to stand behind Eliza, holding a heavy silver tea tray until she decided that she wanted something to drink. She told me that that's what good servants were supposed to do and I might as well learn my place now so I'd be prepared in the future. Other times she'd call me to help her get ready for one of her soirees while Momma was downstairs preparing food, and she'd make me get down on my hands and knees and scrub her feet before massaging lotion onto them. Then she'd make me polish each toenail, cursing me the entire time. If I mistakenly got polish on her skin, she'd pinch me on the soft baby flesh under my arms and spit in my face, telling me that I was as worthless as my mother. Over and over, she'd humiliated me and hurt me in my youth and I'd said nothing. Now here I was a young woman, scarred and haunted by those memories, and I was ready to speak out. But how could I? Who could I tell? Momma was dead, and my father was long gone, too. What actions could I take that would dignify me and make up for the rotten things she'd done to me?

The next week I still didn't have any answers, but nonetheless I called Justin Randolph, agreeing to take whatever was left. I'd lost this time, but I refused to ever lose again. Whatever was mine I'd claim. And I started with my name. That day I combined John Freeman's moniker for me with my father's name, and I buried Claudia Fryar. That day I became Peach Harrison.

11

Cotton is probably one of the most underrated fabrics. It's breathable, it's dependable, and it can be woven into beautiful knits. In fact, woven tightly or loosely, finished smoothly or coarsely, it can take on the look of just about any other fabric, and its durability means that it can stand up to just about anything.

Momma was like that. Though strained, I'm sure, from carrying the weighty burden of the paternity of her child, she put on a good face, working hard for the Harrisons while also accommodating her dressmaking clientele. Though at times she seemed tired, she never complained about her predicament, perhaps because she'd made her choice about whom she would love and accepted the consequences of bearing her married employer's child. She simply moved forward, trying to make progress. That's how come she missed so much of what was happening to me, and that's why she didn't see the beginning of Louis Harrison vanishing before her eyes.

When I was fifteen, I had my first inkling that something was amiss with my father. It began with what seemed like a stubborn cold that he just couldn't shake. It took up residence in the upper part of his chest, not low enough to cause phlegm to take hold, nor high enough for the stuffy, cloudy feeling to invade his head. He just cleared his throat constantly and gulped down the honey, lemon, onion, and brandy concoction Momma prepared, laughingly calling it Momma's Geechee Brew. He couldn't be persuaded to go to the doctor; instead, he shrugged the sickness off, calling it simply a lingering cold.

Worry lines crept onto Momma's full face, but she did nothing. Until she noticed obscene amounts of wasted dinner in the kitchen trash can when she arrived at work in the morning. She wasn't sure, at first, who was wasting the food, but then she noticed my father's thin face looking more gaunt than she was used to. At our house she prepared foods from his youth, trying to lure back his appetite, but it was to no avail.

"Not hungry, Georgia," he would say and move out of the kitchen, then he'd try to distract her and amuse me with lively tales of his childhood.

Momma would laugh and smile, but she still looked worried.

Although he was always dapper, his suits began to hang differently on his thinning frame. Momma altered them, but when she complained about his weight loss, he simply went to his tailor in Germantown to have more suits made.

His workday shortened, and he spent time nestled into

a Queen Anne chair in his home office, reading quietly or listening to jazz. With a drink by his side, he'd pass his days without much fanfare until it was time to take us home.

Eliza finally convinced him to go to the hospital. There the heart disease that had gone undetected too long, coupled with a spirit of defeat at not being able to make his own decisions and run his life and business anymore, seemed to force him into the coma in which he remained for a month. He died the week after my sixteenth birthday. His funeral was a dignified affair—no whooping or yelling from the mourners, just subtle swipes at the eyes with monogrammed linen handkerchiefs by people who, to me, seemed too calm to have really cared about him. At the church there was a formal, catered repast, but after that close friends and family gathered at the Harrison home in what seemed more like a tea party. The guests seemed to have forgotten why they were there as they raided my father's liquor cabinet while his wife pretended to look stricken in between the jokes she told. Disgusted, I helped Momma as she moved through the house collecting crystal shot glasses, goblets, and china to be washed and dried immediately, for Eliza never liked the look of dishes drying on the rack.

After the last guest left, Eliza stood in the kitchen with her arms folded across her balloonlike breasts. She watched as Momma wiped the counter and I swept the floor. I was very conscious of Eliza's presence as I focused on imaginary dust in the corner.

She unfolded her right arm, revealing a hand thick with folded bills.

"I don't ever want to see you again," she said flatly as she placed the money on the counter that Momma had just wiped. Though her voice was without emotion, her eyes raged with fire.

Momma stopped wiping and looked up, rubbing her hands on the apron that covered her large thighs. She didn't look shocked or angry, only sad.

"Either one of you," Eliza hissed, her eyes falling on me.

"You've made a fool of me for years, both of you. But no more. Leave my home," she said before turning slowly and walking out of the kitchen and across the hardwood floor, the click of her heels echoing behind her.

Momma looked down at the floor, and for a moment I thought that a tear would fall. But it didn't. I knew that she missed Louis Harrison. She'd depended on him in so many ways. So had I. For all practical purposes, he'd been my father, though it hadn't been confirmed to me yet. But now that he was gone, I felt a void that made me ache. I know that Momma did, too. Instead of crying, she took off her apron and folded it before placing it on the counter. Then she took the folded bills in one hand and my hand in the other, and together we walked back to our Roslyn Street house.

With her primary source of income gone, Momma placed calls to all her clients over the next few weeks to see if they were interested in her new designs. Some did not return her calls. Those she caught at home responded with a flat no and hung up without explanation or apology. Their loyalties lay decidedly with Eliza.

Momma spent a few weeks working with Mamie. She'd rise before the sun, shower, then don a pair of black slacks and a white blouse and pull her hair back into a bun before creeping into my room to kiss me good-bye. I'd hear the floor creak as she made her way downstairs to the kitchen, where she whipped up breakfast and left it wrapped in foil for me to eat before school. Then she'd tiptoe out the door and head down to the restaurant. Side by side, she and Miss Mamie would dish up southern cuisine smothered in laughter with a side of hospitality, but cooking was Miss Mamie's dream, not Momma's. She'd already experienced a life in which her sewing needle brought her not only pleasure but also profit, and it was hard as hell going back to life without fulfillment.

She came home one evening, rubbing her head and sighing heavily. I suspected that she was having yet another headache, which she tried to hide from me but I always saw. I dutifully gave her aspirin and a glass of water. The sigh had told a story as well. In it were the spent hope, the lost dreams, and the wasted emotions that Philadelphia had meant for her. Without verbalizing it, I knew that she wanted to leave the city, to start over somewhere else. She would just fold away her designing dreams, pack them away neatly, and unfold them again in a new place. A different place.

But I never dreamed that Moultrie, Georgia, her hometown, would be that place.

For the four years we lived in Georgia, she struggled, licking her wounds and trying to inspire others while making a living with her love of fashion. She and I would high-step around town in some of her tailored pieces, accentuated by hats and costume jewelry, hoping to draw attention to Momma's haute-couture designs. Despite our best efforts, our two-woman fashion shows didn't take. The locals thought us pretentious, even a bit odd, so Momma did the only work she could get—alterations on some garments, laundering and pressing others—never returning to designing and sewing in the manner that she loved.

Day in and day out, she worked feverishly, beginning at 4 a.m., pressing clothes that she hand-delivered to customers with a smile by 8. The next five hours were spent washing clothes, and while they dried she modified clients' apparel, hemming cuffs, adding extra panels of fabric in under the arms to make some garments roomier. She did all this to pay for my college education. I didn't know then about my father's will—I didn't find out about that until years later. All I knew was that my mother, who was always hardy, was now being wracked by some physical ailment, and with no health benefits, she attempted to heal herself. But it was of no use.

Every now and then she'd rush to the bathroom and vomit up her guts, blaming it on her nerves. And every now and then I'd see her face contorted with pain, as if she was experiencing the worst headache of her life. I'd give her a few aspirin, hoping that they'd do the trick. But the aneurysm that was secretly and slowly claiming her would not be quieted by a few aspirin.

It ruptured one day when I had late classes at Moultrie State and a study group. When I came home, close to midnight, I found her slumped over her sewing machine. I never knew what her last thoughts or words were, and I prayed that my name wasn't the last thing on her lips. If it was, the guilt that consumed me would have been too great. That I, her sometimes thoughtless, often brooding daughter, had not been there for her in her dying moments. Instead of directing my anger, despair, and hopelessness toward myself, I turned it onto the ones who had driven her away from the place she loved, the place she had settled to make a life and a home. And with a daughter's rage, I vowed to get revenge.

12

During the two hectic weeks before the Camden Academy silent auction, Ishmael called me to check in so often that it felt like a comfortable routine into which seasoned couples settled. I chattered about my day, giving him the heads-up on guests I planned to interview on the show, as well as on interesting books I happened upon while researching show ideas.

He talked about the last-minute details of the auction that, though small, were taking up too much of his time.

"I can't wait until all this is over," he admitted, with fatigue creeping into his voice.

"Me either. Then I can spend some time getting to know you better," I said boldly.

"Why not get started now?" he asked, and I could almost hear the smile crossing his face.

From there, we settled into another conversation in which we dissected ourselves, sharing our dreams and fears. Both of us desired prosperity. Both of us wanted to make a mark on the world. Both of us wanted to do work and live lives that would have made our mothers proud. When I talked to him, I was overcome by a sense of calm, which was a foreign feeling for me. For years, I'd been driven by the underdog pressure to prove my worth to myself and to others. I'd been relentless, wired, and diligent in my quest, which sometimes seemed like a fruitless battle since I couldn't shake the thoughts of worthlessness that dogged me from my youth. But with him I wanted simply to be me. I wanted to be innocent and carefree. I wanted to be the Claudia that would have existed without the interference of Eliza and the others. But being Claudia came with too much baggage that I wasn't able to unload yet.

Still, I took solace in the relationship that was blossoming between us. Besides my clandestine liaison with John Freeman, I had no real map to follow as far as relationships went, so I was guided by instinct, which told me to immerse myself in his love. And over the ensuing weeks I did. Ordering picnic lunches to be delivered to his office at Camden Academy, which the two of us ate after I came off the set. Meeting on Kelly Drive for six-mile walks that passed in an instant as we meandered along the river side by side. Helping him sort boxes of new books and supplies that had been delivered for the teachers at the school. Spending rainy Saturday afternoons in my apartment, with nothing to interrupt our conversations for hours at a time. I thought of him constantly and gazed at his pictures, which were posted in key spots in my home, at work, and even in my car. I kept one of his T-shirts tucked away in my desk at work, and I stopped to inhale his scent whenever I needed a fix. He wore Burberry Touch cologne, and the mix of its scent with his natural smell was branded into my olfactory memory. My time with Ishmael was magical, and the magic of it amazed me. All the advice columns and talk shows warned against jumping headfirst into romantic relationships the way we had. But Ishmael was more than just a romantic relationship. He was my obsession.

But I had one more that gnawed at my gut.

I still hurt from the years of humiliation by Eliza Harrison, and the wounded little girl in me still had to prove my worthiness to her specifically and her kind in general. The Inner Circle interview was the first test Peach Harrison had to face.

On the morning of the interview, I found myself plagued with anxiety as I tried to get dressed, muttering curses and wondering why I'd been stupid enough to agree to talk to Eliza, especially given her parting words to me and Momma before running us out of town. The thought of meeting her face-to-face again was terrifying, and as I paced back and forth I was considering calling my producer and backing out when the mirror in the foyer caught my eye. As I walked toward it the image I saw in my mind was the me that I normally projected to the world: confident, radiant, sophisticated, and attractive. It didn't match the sullen, puffy-eyed woman in the mirror, whose mane of stunning curls was pulled back into a frizzy ponytail.

Studying the image, I found the radiant me beginning to speak.

"Peach, you have no business being nervous about seeing Eliza Harrison today. She doesn't rule you. They aren't any better than you are, and they never have been. Look at what you've done with your life. You've broken down all the synthetic barriers that people like them built. You're one of the most respected, best-looking, highest-paid newscasters in this city. You host a hit show, live in a great place, and have a good man who really digs you. You need to stop your sniveling, lift your chin up, and put your best foot forward. You're a queen. So what, you weren't born in a palace. You live in one now, and it doesn't matter how you got there. Now enjoy it."

Studying my reflection in the mirror, I reviewed the words in my head and tried to imbibe them. I settled for giving myself a semblance of a smile before hurrying off to the bedroom to get dressed.

The morning news was a breeze, and I got through it without feeling the pangs of anxiety I thought I would feel as the time crept closer. Between shows I squeezed in a phone call to Ishmael before my briefing with Diana. Although Ishmael knew that I was nervous about an interview, he didn't exactly know why. I didn't want him to see me as the vulnerable kid I'd been or the vengeful adult I'd grown into, so I said nothing.

He talked about how some of the pre-auction publicity the school had received for the auction had garnered some pretty sizable donations.

"That's great, Ish," I remarked. "The school should make a ton of money from this."

"I hope so. I'm so tired that I'm running on pure adrenaline now."

"You'll be able to rest soon," I reassured him.

"Yeah, I can't wait. Still nervous about the show?"

"A little," I confided.

"Don't be. You'll do a good job."

"Thanks," I responded, trying to absorb his optimism. "I'll see you this evening."

"Looking forward to it."

When I hung up, I read my notes for the show and went in search of Diana for my briefing. As I strutted down the halls confidently, nodding to my colleagues, my insides quaked. The closer I got to the set, the more I felt like the little girl who'd spent a lifetime on the outside looking in. And I'd definitely had my fill of looking in at the members of The Inner Circle.

Aside from Elicia and Lindsay, Elizabeth and Louise's daughters, I'd known other kids who were in the organization. One of them was Zola Robbins from Cecilian Academy, the private girls' school I'd attended, and I got a rush out of every Inner Circle outing she invited me to.

Despite the fact that my pedigree didn't fit her mother's standards, Zola genuinely liked me, so she tried to include me as much as possible. I liked her, too, but more than that, I envied her. Without having to work for it at all, she had built-in connections with the movers and shakers not only in Philadelphia but in the more than two hundred cities across the country where The Inner Circle had chapters. I resented that I was prevented from joining despite the fact that I was intelligent, articulate, and talented. So I simply did the next best thing: I got as close to her as possible, so that even if I couldn't officially gain entrée into that world, I would at least know its rules.

From the way Zola's mother, Mrs. Robbins, glared at me in the rearview mirror when I was a kid whenever she picked me up for an event, it was obvious that she merely tolerated me. It was as if she was afraid that I'd stink up her Jaguar. I used syrupy sweetness to counteract her hostility, and I went on about my way, absorbing the lessons of The Inner Circle elite.

The trips I took with The Inner Circle were educationally and culturally relevant. One weekend we went to New York, where we visited the Schomburg Center for Research in Black Culture, the Studio Museum in Harlem, and the Apollo Theater. We ate lunch at Sylvia's and had dinner at Gracie Mansion, hosted by the mayor himself, whose chief of staff was a Spelman alum with children active in The Inner Circle's New York City chapter.

Another weekend we went on a tour of Maryland and Virginia colleges, visiting Morgan State, Howard, Virginia Union, and Hampton. At Hampton we went sailing on the president's yacht. His wife, a member of the Richmond area chapter, had arranged for the sunset tour, which took us into the Chesapeake Bay.

Yet another weekend found us exploring our own backyard as we visited sites key to the Underground Railroad and the abolition movement. We saw Mother Bethel A.M.E., the church founded by the remarkable Richard Allen, who purchased his freedom and went on to assist others in doing so.

These were opportunities I would never have had on my own. It was no wonder that few kids like me were ever able to make the transition from a station of poverty to one of privilege. I'd admired those who were able to do it, and I'd planned to continue using Zola as long as I could to get the results that I wanted. But things didn't happen that way. When we were about to graduate from eighth grade,

Zola's mother made up her mind that I was unworthy of her daughter's friendship, and she forbade her to associate with me anymore. Although I was never given a firm reason why our friendship was being dismantled, I assumed that it was because my pedigree wasn't suitable for the real, meaningful interaction that high school would include. Because we lived far apart and wouldn't be attending the same high school, Zola acquiesced, and that was the end of the friendship. Even though I'd been using her as a tool for my advancement, the death of that friendship really hurt me, because it was one more blow to my already fragile self-confidence.

The emotional pain that had dogged me from all the childhood exclusion and humiliation made me want to find some way to humiliate Eliza, and as I sat in the makeup chair, watching a news brief detailing an ongoing investigation into some celebrity scandal, I was reminded of the power of my position. People knew me as the bright, perky reporter who was fair but determined, so I decided to simply hand Eliza the shovel and shine a light on her as she dug her own grave.

Eliza and Bertha Norman, the national president of the organization, sat on the set, getting miked, chatting with each other, and looking self-important, as I spoke with Diana. Always impeccably dressed, Eliza wore a lavender silk pantsuit with gunmetal spike heels. Her platinum-and-diamond necklace dripped downward into her she-must-be-wearing-a-helluva-bra-because-I-don't-believe-those-girls-still-sit-up-like-that-at-their-age cleavage. Her wavy hair had thinned, but it was still dyed and pulled back into a bun at the base of her neck. She wore large, ridiculous-looking sunglasses, as if she were being stalked by the paparazzi. Bertha Norman, on the other hand, dressed conservatively but elegantly in a navy blue suit. The Hermès scarf draped over her shoulder was the only outward indicator of wealth.

"Those sunglasses might be a problem," I said to Diana, gesturing toward Eliza.

"I know, but she refuses to remove them, so we'll just have to have her sit at an angle and hope that there's no glare," Diana said, sounding as if she'd battled with the grande dame and lost.

"Divas," I said, feigning exasperation.

"You're telling me," she said, smiling.

Taking a deep breath, I walked toward the set, finally ready to meet Eliza face-to-face after all these years. Only Bertha Norman looked up.

"Mrs. Norman, Mrs. Harrison."

Bertha Norman smiled with recognition and said, "What a pleasure." Eliza turned her head awkwardly, and she seemed to be following the sound of my voice for direction.

"Great goodness, she's gone blind," I thought when the realization hit me. Yet and still, there would be no pity, as she had taken none on me. I just had to be careful not to look as if I was beating up on a little old blind lady.

Any bit of sympathy I was tempted to feel dissipated as the show moved on.

In the first segment, Bertha Norman was levelheaded and confident as she discussed the current programming of The Inner Circle and fielded questions from callers about where she'd like to steer the organization during her tenure. She stressed the importance of the community-service hours that each chapter was required to fulfill, explaining that it's very easy for some of the children to feel that their privilege should shield them from the less fortunate. She said that she was determined to develop the humane side of the children in addition to the cultured side.

Between segments, I directed, "Mrs. Harrison, turn toward your left a bit. We don't want the camera to pick up a glare from the lights overhead."

"Thank you for being so understanding," she said, shifting in her seat. "My eyes have gotten so bad with age, and I refuse to have surgery. It just doesn't seem right to have somebody cutting on my eyes. If I have to go blind, at least I'll do it in style," she said and laughed uncomfortably.

"You're a handful," I said, faking amusement at the old bat's vanity.

". . . three, two, one . . ."

"Welcome back. I'm Peach Harrison, and today I'm speaking with Bertha Norman, national president of The Inner Circle, an organization that will be convening in Philadelphia next week to mark its fiftieth anniversary. I'm also joined by Eliza Harrison, who, along with three other women, founded the organization all those years ago. Welcome to the show, Mrs. Harrison."

I gave my best television smile in Eliza's direction, while she, in her darkly tinted shades, looked aloof before pasting a smile on her face.

"It's a pleasure to be here."

"We've been talking about present programming of the organization, but I'd like to know, what did you have in mind when you first conceived the idea for The Inner Circle?"

"Well, I envisioned a selective club that would bring together children of like stations in life so they could socialize with their peers. Their mothers would organize activities in which the children would participate, and the monthly meeting would rotate between members' homes. Membership would span from birth until high school graduation."

"What were the criteria for membership?"

"Prospective members had to be able to afford to participate in the organization's events, but financial status alone would not be enough to guarantee admission. If that were the case, the children of every black numbers runner and bootlegger in town would be able to join. Membership would be by recommendation only, and the members would have the final say as to who would be allowed to join. I served as the first president, and I set the tone so that only the right kind of people were admitted. After all, my children were members, and I certainly didn't want my daughters to associate with just anyone. Besides, providing the community service and cultural enrichment, the organization also served as a pool of potential mates, so that our children would marry people of comparable background. That's what my own daughters did, and they've lived very happy lives surrounded by their own kind."

I battled between cringing and laughing as the damning, classist words tumbled out of Eliza Harrison's mouth. Bertha Norman cleared her throat nervously, ready to jump in and smooth things over diplomatically, but Eliza wouldn't be quieted.

"Interesting. Was there ever a fear that the group would be branded elitist?"

"In the sixties there was a cry for us to be less stringent in our membership requirements and to open our doors to some who didn't fit the traditional mold, but I thought that was just plain silly. Would you ask the Kennedys to let hillbillies into their social clubs? I think not. So we just kept on according to plan, screening the way we'd always done, and that's how we've managed to keep the riffraff out," Eliza rattled on absently.

Bertha butted in, trying to do damage control: "With all due respect to our founder, we have changed quite a bit over the years. That's the only way that an organization will grow. So we've relaxed our standards a bit to reflect a broader representation of African American life."

I smiled wanly before announcing a caller with a comment: "We have Deanna from Kensington on the line. Yes, Deanna."

"Who they think they is, callin' people riffraff and puttin' down regular, hardworkin' people just 'cuz they got a little piece of money. That ain't even right. Miss, I bet if you tilt your nose down some, you'll see that you got some riffraff right in your own family."

"See, listen to them. Just common," Eliza said, sniffing and elevating her nose with an air of superiority.

"Wait," Bertha interjected again, trying to salvage the interview. "It's not the way it sounds."

"Bertha, just whose side are you on, dear? There's no need to backpedal. We know what kind of people we don't want around us. I won't apologize for who I am, and neither should you, Bertha, or anyone who was born privileged."

"That's a very good point, Mrs. Harrison. Do the elite need to apologize for being who they are?" I asked.

"Absolutely not," Eliza said, sitting back in her chair like she was Marie Antoinette.

"I don't think so either, but we certainly don't want the viewers to get the wrong impression of us and our organization," Bertha whined.

"The devil with them," Eliza said, stamping her foot defiantly.

"And on that note, we're out of time. I thank you for being our guests today, Eliza Harrison and Bertha Norman. Your organization, The Inner Circle, will be convening at the Convention Center in Philadelphia in just a few weeks. For more information about the event, visit them at their Web site. Thank you, as always, for tuning in to our show. I'm Peach Harrison, and I look forward to joining you again tomorrow."

Before the set lights could be dimmed, Bertha was on her feet. "How could you do that? I should have known better than to bring you with me, you senile old bat. Do you know what you've done? Our reputation will be ruined."

She turned to me, pleading, "Is there some way that we can edit that?"

"Sorry, Mrs. Norman. It was live," I said, standing.

"Can I have another chance to come on and speak?"

"I'd like to accommodate you, but you'll need to speak with the producer about that."

"Let me see if I can catch her now," she said, flying off the set, leaving Eliza sitting in her seat with a smug look plastered on her face.

"Now, that was interesting," I said to her, removing my microphone.

"I hold my tongue for no one," she said, with an old lady's pride stamped on her face.

"I can see that." I sauntered toward her, knelt down beside her, and leaned in to whisper: "Perhaps it's best to keep your mouth shut sometimes. You never know who you might hurt. You know? Think back. Way back."

"Who do you think you are to tell me what I should and shouldn't say?"

"Actually, I should be asking you that. Who do *you* think I am? It's not hard to figure out."

She looked befuddled as she racked her brain, searching her memory for some clue to my identity.

"Aw, c-c-come on, M-M-Mrs. Harrison," I said, regressing to the stuttering of my childhood. "Did you really think you'd gotten rid of me?"

"Claudia!" she shrieked, her pale face blanching even further.

"Oh, so you *do* know my name, huh?" I mocked, alluding to her careless cruelty all those years ago.

"I'm ba-a-ack," I sang. "You're right. You don't have to see me again, you blind old bitch, but you'll definitely feel my pressure."

With that, I stood up and walked over to the alternate set where my next segment would take place. When I looked over my shoulder, the old woman was still sitting there, dumbfounded, with her mouth agape. Then she lifted her chin in a show of superiority, but she had already shown how uncouth she was.

13

The day after my interview with Eliza Harrison was the silent auction for Camden Academy, and my nerves were flustered again but for different reasons. Looking incredibly handsome in a charcoal gray suit and a pale smoke shirt, Ishmael arrived to pick me up three hours before the auction was set to begin. Wearing a strapless black dress accessorized with turquoise jewelry, I took his breath away.

As we drove to Camden, my hand resting on his thigh, we listened to Latin jazz and salsa, our bodies vibrating to the music.

"I didn't know you liked salsa," I commented.

"I grew up hearing it all over Camden. I can't help but like it."

"Can you dance to it?" I asked.

"Is that a real question, or is it a challenge?"

"Take it however you like it."

"Sounds like a challenge to me," he remarked, putting on his turn signal and easing the car toward the curb.

We unbuckled our seatbelts and stared each other down, like opponents ready to do battle. As we got out of the car we continued taking each other in with stoic faces. He grabbed my hand and the dance began.

Hips gyrated, arms guided, hands fluttered and teased as he took the lead, twirling me around the sidewalk as the music blared. With our eyes locked, our bodies danced with passion, and when we finished, both of our bodies glistened with perspiration. He leaned me back against the car, kissing me hungrily, and I knew that we'd never make it to the auction on time.

Moments later, we were back at my apartment, tearing at each other's clothes and littering the hallway with them. We made it as far as the living room, and there our bodies consumed each other's in rapturous waves. Spent, we drifted into a light sleep before showering and making a second attempt to get to the Camden Aquarium, and we arrived a few minutes ahead of the first attendee.

Ishmael was determined and driven, and he never saw obstacles. He only saw challenges, and he thought of them as hurdles to build his momentum. He and Isaac truly worked as a team, weighing the pros and cons of every new venture, hammering out all kinds of problems together. When I watched them work together, I was a little envious that I didn't have a sibling to balance me out in the same way.

"He's literally my other half," Ishmael explained one early evening when he joined me at my apartment for dinner. "It's weird to explain, but even when we disagree, it's like just seeing the other side of the coin. You know? We just kind of help each other see the whole picture."

"Is there ever a time when you don't see eye to eye?" I inquired.

He was pensive for a moment before responding with a laugh. "Not really. I mean, he's me, and I don't really get mad at myself."

"You're right. That is weird."

"Don't you ever wish that you had somebody else, like a sister or something?"

"I used to. Things would have been much easier if I'd been able to lean on somebody else. Or even bounce ideas off of someone else. I might have made some different choices."

"Like what, Claudia? You sound like you have some regrets."

"I don't really think of them as regrets. I did the best I could with what I had. If things had been different, I would have done things differently."

"You make it sound like your life was really hard," he commented, tracing a finger over my thigh.

"Well, it wasn't the hardest, but it wasn't easy. Yeah, I knew my dad, unlike you guys, but he was my mom's boss, and his real family, his legitimate family, didn't take too kindly to me."

This was my first time revealing that much about my childhood to anyone, and I wasn't sure how deeply I wanted to delve. I didn't know how much I could say, because the emotional scars, though inflicted long ago, were still raw. That was why I was still on my quest for revenge. But Ishmael, with his heart and benevolent spirit, though shrouded in street survival camouflage, wouldn't understand that.

163

"What?" he fished, questioning my silence.

"What what?" I replied.

"What aren't you saying?"

"We have time to get to know what each other's silences mean," I responded.

"No time like the present."

I weighed my options quickly, wondering what in my emotional warehouse he'd find acceptable and what he'd find objectionable. I didn't want to scare him off, so I chose the safe route.

"I was also a pudgy kid with a slight stutter and crooked teeth."

"Now, that I don't believe."

"It's true. That's why you don't remember me from college. I was pretty unremarkable. I got braces late in high school, and I started seeing a speech therapist. I didn't lose weight until college. That's not that long ago, so that's why I'm so neurotic about what I eat. I can't afford even one extra calorie."

"Oh, yeah." He smiled, leaning toward me.

"Yeah," I replied, returning his smile.

"Would you like to burn a few more calories right now?"

"I think I'm open to it," I said, parting my legs and lying back to give him room.

"And one, two, three . . . ," he chanted quickly as he leaned down to kiss my neck.

We both had demanding schedules, and sometimes work threatened to encroach on our weekends together. Sometimes we gave in and I spent Saturdays with him at the school. Or he spent Saturday mornings on my sofa while I flipped through newspapers and magazines searching for stories that begged for exploration and coverage. Despite our hectic schedules, we vowed never to work on Sundays. That was our day to block out the world and focus on each other. Sundays usually began with an early morning service with Isaac at a Baptist church in Camden. Ishmael liked to stay grounded in faith and connected with the community, so he was pleased to run into some of his students in church.

"Always teaching," he'd say when his students approached him with smiles after service. He wanted them to see that his willingness to show submission to a greater force made him more of a man, not less. That was fine for him, but I always had to fight the childish urge to squirm throughout the service. It wasn't that I didn't enjoy the music. In fact, some of the most powerful, soul-shaking songs I ever heard were belted out by vocalists from right there in that Camden church. It wasn't that I didn't enjoy fellowship. In fact, meeting some of those down-to-earth, regular folks reminded me of my own sweet, beloved Momma. It was the messages that didn't sit well with me. It seemed like the preacher, Reverend Basilio Bettiford, a handsome young half-black, half–Puerto Rican powerhouse who reminded me of Ron "Boriqua Soul" Juarez, had an inside track on my brain. His sermons were always pointed, and as his eyes flashed over the culturally diverse congregation, I could have sworn that they lingered on me more than on the others. Every week he spoke on a variety of topics from adultery, saying "You cheat God when you cheat on your spouse," to self-preservation: "Knowing when to walk away from a godless person."

"God's the maker of all things," the minister proclaimed, chuckling, from the pulpit one Sunday. "And if He made everything, then you know that He knows its content, inside and out. My daddy used to say that you can't put a silk shirt on a pig. That's because sooner or later that pig's nature is going to come out, and it's going to soil that silk. It's the same thing with us, my brothers and sisters. Brothers, you can hide behind layers of expensive clothing that make you look and feel bigger than you are. Sisters, you can paint up that outside in M.A.C. or Chanel. Some of y'all are looking at me like, 'How does he know about that?' You forget that my lovely wife is from the other side of Camden County. She knows the pretty side. Me? I'm from here, so I know the not-so-pretty side. I know that beneath the Chanel can be a heart as ugly as they come. But you've got to remember that the heart wasn't born ugly. God created it, so it is inherently beautiful. You've got to get back to that beauty. Peel off those layers of ostracism and criticism, poverty and pain. They weren't born in you. That's other people's stuff. Those are their burdens. But you don't have to pick them up. Stand naked and empty-handed before God, and he'll take you right back in."

That message, which he delivered on Easter, had pecked away at my psyche, and as we left church I reached out to shake his hand as he stood in the vestibule after the benediction.

"Thank you for those words," I said, pumping his hand as Ishmael and Isaac stood in the vestibule talking to students.

"Thank you for hearing them," he said, smiling benevolently.

I needed to tell him how much they had hit home, so I continued: "You're right. It is easier to hide beneath layers of stuff, material or otherwise."

Cupping my hand between his, he leaned in closer and

lowered his voice: "That's why it's important to get na-ked . . . before God."

I drew back and searched his face for signs of double en-tendre that I thought I heard in his voice. His eyes twinkled, and he was all smiles again.

Disappointed, I withdrew my hand, and I headed out to meet Ishmael and Isaac.

After church we usually dropped Isaac off and headed to brunch at a restaurant of my choosing in Philadelphia. This week, Isaac and a companion joined us as we enjoyed the brunch buffet at a Center City hotel restaurant. With memo-ries of my pudgy days imprinted on my fat cells, I usually avoided buffets like the plague, but in an effort to accom-modate everyone, I strayed from my big plate, little food, big price norm.

The four of us sat by a window overlooking a fountain in the lobby. Isaac's date, Kim, sat next to me, while the twins sat across from us facing the door. "Some old bad habits are hard to shake," Isaac explained with a wry chuckle, refer-ring to his past illegal enterprise.

"We all have those," I replied, looking at Kim, who was taking out a compact and checking her reflection again.

It was the fifth time she'd done it since we left church. She was an attractive girl, but she was definitely not an intellec-tual. I wouldn't have thought that Isaac, with his serious de-meanor, would have been attracted to someone as vain and shallow as Kim was, but she probably balanced him out in some way. The light to his heavy, the fluff to his brooding.

Whatever it was, he doted on this shallow woman, pull-ing out her chair, rising every time she looked as if she was going to stand up.

As usual, Ishmael was also attentive, just in a different way. He always offered me a seat at the table of intellect; we would discuss, debate, and even fight about current events, political philosophy, and who played a better trumpet, the contemporary Freddie Hubbard or the standard-setter Dizzy Gillespie. Today's "battle" was no different, and as we charted the growth and changes in reggae as it compared to rap, Kim looked befuddled while Isaac looked amused.

As we chatted our conversation meandered along whichever road someone chose. Warmth and comfort washed over me as I sat back, surveying the room. That's when I spotted them.

Thomas and Elizabeth Harrison Brooks sat with another couple at a table on the other side of the room. I hadn't seen them in years. Time seemed to have left Thomas relatively unmolested. Elizabeth, on the other hand, looked a little fuller in the face, though she was never a small woman to begin with. I saw Thomas stand and walk toward the door, heading toward the hotel's lobby, and I stood, too.

"Too many mimosas," I said, excusing myself.

Walking through the lobby, I spied him in the window of the smoker's lounge, lighting up. His back was to me as I glided past, heading toward the ladies' room. I checked my reflection, powdered my face, and added a layer of lip gloss to my full, succulent lips. Pleased with my image, I walked back to the lobby.

Standing outside the smokers' lounge, I made a big to-do of looking for something in my purse, dropping it in hopes that the sudden movement would get Thomas's attention. I wasn't disappointed. As I knelt, quickly gathering my belongings, I looked up in a show of fake embarrassment, and I saw that he was part of my audience. I gave a quick smile, and he reciprocated. Then he walked to an ashtray, snuffed out his cigarette, and exited the lounge. In the lobby he smiled at me again before asking, "How do I know you?"

"You probably wake up with me every morning," I replied suggestively.

He flushed before the click of realization lit him. "Peach Harrison."

"In the flesh."

"Good to meet you," he said, offering his hand.

"I'll say that the pleasure is mine as soon as you tell me your name," I responded, feigning ignorance.

"I'm Thomas Brooks," he said, digging into his breast pocket and retrieving a business card.

"Well, it's definitely a pleasure, counselor," I said, alluding to the Esquire behind his name.

"You recently interviewed someone I know."

"Oh? Who was that?"

"My mother-in-law, one of the founders of The Inner Circle."

"Oh," I said, twisting my lips into a semblance of a sympathetic smile. "The interview went well, but she said some pretty, uh, interesting things."

He smiled. "You're telling me. They even had a few picketers outside the convention. My wife was so upset she almost had a conniption. She kept saying that she couldn't believe you would stoop so low as to do that to her poor blind old mother."

"Interesting. I was just doing my job. It was Mrs. Harrison's own comments that did the damage. Oh, well, I guess you need to be sure to keep our meeting today a secret," I said, winking.

"I will," he replied conspiratorially.

We headed back into the dining room, where we smiled at each other before going our separate ways.

As I sat back down Ishmael said, "You were gone awhile. I was about to come after you."

"No need, sweetness. I just got stopped by a fan."

Later that night in my apartment I twirled the cream business card over and over in my hand, studying the gold and black print. Thomas Brooks had always been kind to me on the rare occasions when I was in his company. Maybe it was because, as a self-made, first-generation attorney, he knew what it was like to be an outsider. Maybe it was because he knew what a bitch his wife could be. Whatever the reason, I planned to get a little closer to Thomas Brooks, Esquire.

14

"Hi. This is Peach Harrison," I said into the receiver.

"Peach, thanks so much for calling so quickly," Suzanne Berry, editor in chief of *The Philadelphia Ledger*, said.

"Sure. Rich Thompkins is a good friend, and he told me that you wanted to connect with me," I remarked, clicking the tip of my Cross pen.

"Right. I want to talk to you about an opportunity."

"Suzanne, I'm sure you know that it would be a breach of contract for me to work for any other media outlets."

"Of course," she responded, unruffled. "I'd like to speak with you face-to-face about the opportunity I have in mind. When's a good time for us to meet?"

"I'm actually leaving the station now, and I have a hole in my schedule before an appointment this evening," I said, looking at my nails. Ivana, my manicurist, was squeezing me in before she left for her cruise that evening.

"Great. Let's meet for coffee at Jerky Joe's. How's a half hour?"

"That's good. See you then."

I hung up, wondering what I could have that Suzanne Berry could possibly want.

Thirty minutes later, I was sipping green tea, listening to her explain an idea she said had been rattling around in her head for the past month.

"The column, called The Social Butterfly, would be similar to the society columns of old but a little edgier. Because you'd be writing under a pseudonym, you could feel free to catch the ladies who lunch doing their good deeds, but you could also dish the dirt about the moneyed matrons and mistresses. You're a recognizable face, and many of them would love to get close to you, be counted among your friends. From what I understand, you're already moving in some rare-air circles. They'll grant you access to their lives, and in turn you'll grant readers that same access."

"Isn't that a bit unscrupulous?"

"Peach, it's journalism. A lot of what we do is considered unscrupulous by many, yet they can't turn their eyes away."

"Well, the pay sounds good, and so do the perks, but I need your assurance that my name won't ever get out, because that's a contractual violation, and it would mean my job," I said, intrigued but cautious.

"You have my pledge."

"Let me think about it, and I'll get back to you before the week is over?"

"Great." Suzanne smiled, shaking my hand.

"We don't have a deal yet," I cautioned.

"I'm just glad that you're considering it."

I certainly didn't need any more on my plate, which was already full with Ishmael, work, and the occasional social event. But as I considered Suzanne's offer I thought about how it could advance me both professionally and socially. I was already receiving tons of invitations to attend or cover high-profile, black-tie events through work. "This," I reasoned, "is merely an extension of my primary job." Nobody, including Ishmael, would have to know that I was, in essence, a double agent.

In addition to advancing myself professionally and socially, I'd have the chance to use my pen as a sword, thrashing those who'd wronged me and Momma in the past. It wasn't just the Harrisons, although Eliza was the one to seal the deal. There were all those clients—the wives of CEOs, politicians, and entrepreneurs—whom Momma had dutifully serviced with the beautifully crafted garments she made for them. They swore that she was the de la Renta of Philadelphia. In the end, they showed where their loyalties lay.

I had watched Momma sitting by the telephone in our West Oak Lane house. She'd made call after call, each beginning the same way.

"Good day. Mrs. So and So, please," she'd say. "Hi, this is Georgia Fryar, how are you? Good . . . good. Look, I wanted you to know that I've just finished some new designs, and I had you in mind when I sketched one of them. When can I come over and show it to you? . . . Really, it won't take long. . . . You could stop by here if it's more convenient for you. I know how busy you are. . . . But, really, they're lovely, just lovely. . . . Okay . . . well, give me a call when you're interested. Let me give you my number. . . . Okay. I'll look to hear from you."

She could have stayed in Philly and thrived as a designer if only these women had had backbones and hadn't been so cliquish. She wouldn't have had to return to Moultrie, trying to make the best of a broken soul.

After considering what I could gain by assaulting them in the press the way they'd assaulted my mother's pride, I called Suzanne and told her that I'd accept the position. The minor embarrassment I caused Eliza on *Around Philly* was nothing compared to what I'd do as The Social Butterfly.

"So how would you like to relax on something like this?" I asked Ishmael as we walked on the polished deck of a sixty-foot 560 Express by Cruisers Yachts. I'd talked him into coming to the Atlantic City Boat Show with me for an outing one weekend. I had no intention of purchasing a boat just yet, but I thought it would be fun to explore the possibilities.

"It would definitely be a nice change of pace."

"Nice is hardly the word," I nearly whispered, afraid that if I spoke too loudly, I'd snap out of the dreaminess that filled me as I took in the view of the cabin.

"This living room is bigger than the one in our childhood home in Camden."

I smiled knowingly. I had grown up in a sliver of a house that was flanked closely by other slivers of houses. I took his hand, and we walked through the kitchen to the sleeping quarters. The spacious master bedroom was equipped with its own flat-screen television and a state-of-the-art audio system. Unlike in some of the other boats we'd seen, this one's master bedroom had its own large bathroom, with a shower large enough to accommodate two comfortably.

"Let's try it out," Ish suggested, reading my thoughts.

As we slid in, wrapping our arms around each other, I heard voices approaching.

"Okay, okay," a male voice was saying, acquiescing.

"Wonderful! I'll get the salesman," the woman said excitedly.

We stepped out of the shower just as the man was entering the master bedroom.

"It sounds like we're encroaching on your territory," I said to the man, whose tanned face broke into a grin when he saw us.

"Almost. The deal's about to be sealed."

"Congratulations," Ishmael said, extending his hand. "She's beautiful."

"So's she," the dark-haired stranger replied, smiling at me. "Even more so in person."

I smiled as Ishmael put a protective arm around me. "Yup, I say that every morning when I wake up to her."

"Lucky bastard," the man said, smiling.

"Your fortune's not so bad."

"Yeah, you're right about that," he replied, looking around. "I'm Ted Bancroft."

"Ishmael Taylor," Ish returned before turning to me. "And you obviously know Miss Harrison."

I shook hands, smiling. "Ted, congratulations."

Just then his wife blew in with a salesman in tow.

"Meet my wife, Paula."

"Hi, Paula," I said to the smiling brown woman.

"It's wonderful meeting you," she said, beaming.

"Congratulations," I replied, nodding and looking around the boat.

"Oh, I'm so excited! I'm going to christen it and have a little shindig next week. You two have to come."

"We'd love to," I said, looking at Ishmael, who looked a bit vexed.

"Of course, I need to check our calendars first," I amended.

"Okay," Paula replied.

"Do a quick walk-through with us," Ted said, nudging Ishmael with his elbow.

"Well, we really should be headed back to the AC Expressway," Ishmael countered.

"I need someone to share my good fortune with. Come on," Ted urged.

"Yeah, Ish. What's fifteen minutes?"

His eyes flashed at me, then he moved to follow Ted in reluctant acquiescence. He was silent as we moved about the boat, climbing up past the deck to behold the view from above. When we returned to the deck, a smiling salesman awaited Ted and Paula.

"You're going to have some good times here," I said, hoping that my energy projected over Ishmael's quiet brooding. What was the matter with him anyway?

"I hope you'll be joining us at least next week," Paula said, smiling at Ishmael in an attempt to thaw his sudden iciness.

"I'll try," he said, still a bit withdrawn.

"Okay, we'll let you get to your paperwork. Please be in touch," I said, slipping Paula my card.

"Will do."

"Take care," Ted said.

"Take it easy," Ish said, shaking Ted's hand as we disembarked.

"Bye, now," Paula called, looking at home already as she folded herself under her husband's arm.

Ishmael's silence told me that he was finished being social for the day and that we were probably heading home. But before we left, I wanted to know what had gotten in his craw.

"What's on your mind?" I asked as we headed toward the parking lot where my Mercedes was parked.

"Nothing," he said, taking my keys from his pocket. "Here, you drive your car."

I detected intended emphasis on the word *your.*

"Did I do something wrong?"

"Nope. As usual, you were your normal peachy self," he said, standing by the passenger door.

"Is that supposed to mean something?" I asked, feeling fire in my chest.

"Not a thing. Now be a peach and drive home," he quipped, only he wasn't smiling.

On the ride home, the car was filled only with the sound of Stevie Wonder.

Over the ensuing week, Ishmael made his check-in calls, but they were devoid of the vibrant electricity that usually flowed between us. With work and the added responsibility of my society gossip column, I didn't press the issue, because I was swamped. But by Friday evening I couldn't stand the distance between us, so I called him as I finished getting dressed for Ted and Paula's party.

"So you're going without me?" he asked.

"Yes. You didn't seem too interested in being around them for some reason, but I actually like them," I said, which was only half true. Paula had been really nice, but Ted was, while pleasant, a bit creepy with all his constant grinning. Despite that, I knew that I should attend the party for networking purposes, because the people I assumed would be present would be fodder for the column. I'd already mentioned Ted and Paula's names to Suzanne, and it turns out that she's a high-powered attorney and he's a sports agent. Suzanne pretty much ordered me to go. As much as anyone can order Peach Harrison to do anything.

"But my question is, are you really willing to go without me?"

"Do you want to come?"

"No."

"Well, I've already told Paula that I'm coming."

"So call her and tell her that you can't come."

"She's already there, I'm sure, and I have only her home number."

"So just don't go."

"I can't do that."

"Why not?"

"Because that's bad manners. People prepare for an expected number of guests."

"Well, excuse me for not being up on my etiquette. I'm just a teacher from Camden."

"What? You're far more than that. Ishmael, please understand. I have to go to this thing, but I'll come by after it's over. Where is this coming from? Why don't you just come with me?"

"I don't fit in on some guy's sixty-foot yacht. I drive a Honda, not a Mercedes. Come to think of it, maybe I don't fit in with you either. I don't have fans or anything, and nobody watches to see what I'm wearing," he snapped, referring to a recent article in *Philadelphia* magazine that had named me

178

"The Tempting, Trendy Television Personality" among their thirty under thirty.

"Ishmael," I said, sighing, "you do important work, real work that shapes the future. What could be more satisfying than that? It doesn't matter what you drive or wear."

He was quiet, I guess contemplating my words. "So are you going to come over later and be with your man?"

"As soon as I finish," I promised.

"I guess I have to wait," he said, giving in.

"It'll be worth it," I said, glad to have smoothed over this unexpected episode.

"Alright. See you when you get here."

Smiling, I hung up, grabbed my purse, and headed for the door in one seamless motion.

The lights of Atlantic City twinkled in the distance in front of me. Behind me, four NBA players and their flavor-of-the-month companions schmoozed with a cosmetic surgeon, a jeweler, an aspiring model, an artist, an investment banker, a restaurateur, and a few attorneys. Thomas Brooks was among them, and he was alone.

So far he had been involved in numerous conversations that had kept him occupied for just over an hour, but that was fine by me. Between the female artist and two of the athletes meeting in close, dark quarters, and the model disappearing to a private room and returning with a glazed look in her eyes and powdery white residue on her face, I had more than enough juice for my column. Finally, Thomas nodded and smiled at me from across the deck. Holding my second glass of champagne, I winked back.

"Well, well, well. Look who's here," he said.

"In the flesh. Are you sailing solo this evening?"

"I sure am." He smiled widely and swished the amber fluid around his glass before taking a gulp. "You?"

"*Mm-hmm.*" For me, the fact was regrettable, but for him, being without his wife seemed more like a celebration.

"So how do you know our gracious hosts?" he asked.

"I just met them last week when I was down at the marina looking at boats. What about you?"

"Paula and I went to law school together at Howard. The four of us get together every now and then. But one of my wife's clubs is doing something tomorrow, so she's tying up some loose ends."

"Yeah, I guess it was short notice," I said.

"Whatever it was, thank God for small miracles."

I smirked. "I'll let that pass."

"You don't have to if you don't want to."

Clearing my throat, I smiled. Trouble in paradise. Truthfully, it wasn't surprising. Everything I remembered about Elizabeth Harrison Brooks told me that she was hell on wheels from afar and that she would be even more difficult in a personal relationship. Her husband's comments simply confirmed it.

"So what's your specialty?" I asked, referring to his work.

"Pretty women like you."

"Mr. Brooks," I began coyly, "is that you or the alcohol talking?"

"Maybe it's both."

His glazed eyes and slow smile told me exactly where he wanted our conversation to go. Disgruntled in his marriage, he was more than willing to step out on his wife. His confidence told me that, rather than hold his affairs over her head, he'd simply gloat inwardly, like the sly cat who'd swallowed the canary. With his fit physique, flawless copper-colored skin, almond-shaped eyes, and silvered temples framing a headful of thick, wavy hair, he was definitely distinguished and attractive. And I'd seen his picture in the paper enough to know that he was as powerful as he was connected. Too bad Elizabeth couldn't make him happy.

He extended a crooked elbow to me, inviting me to take in the view of the ocean from a different vantage point. And looking at him, I couldn't discern what was behind the glimmer buried in his laughing eyes, but it certainly was alluring, and I couldn't help but oblige.

15

"**M**iss Mamie, he was putty in my hands," I said after giving her the edited version of my encounter with Thomas Brooks two nights ago on the boat.

"Well, his hellcat wife deserves it," she returned, satisfied at any semblance of a comeuppance that a Harrison would encounter.

"Let me run. I have to get to church," I said, slathering a perfumed body cream on my elbows.

"Okay. Say a prayer for me, too. This old broad ain't gettin' 'round like she used to."

"Please, Miss Mamie. You're more spry than anybody else I know."

"Child, please. I'm just makin' do."

"Whatever. Love you."

"Love you back," she said, hanging up the phone.

I looked in the mirror as I massaged moisturizer into my neck, and I remembered Thomas Brooks's lips as they had explored the soft curve of it. After docking the boat, we slipped off to a hotel. After checking out the sights in the lobby, I met him upstairs, and he was all over me, hungry for sex and starved for the comfort of a beautiful woman's arms. He was a good lover, and as he brought me to the edge of bliss, I couldn't help thinking about what his stupid wife was missing out on. Afterward he told me that he'd never cheated on his wife before, he'd always stayed true to his wedding vows, but he found me so irresistible yet sweet, foreign yet familiar, after watching me every day on television. He asked if he could see me again. I told him that I'd love it, but I had to go now because someone was waiting for me. After a quick shower, I stood in front of the mirror, getting ready for the eighty-minute drive to see Ishmael. I called Thomas's name as I fluffed out my curly, wet hair that would dry on the drive home.

"Yes, my sweet Peach," he'd responded.

"Do I look familiar to you?"

"Of course. I look forward to seeing you every morning."

"Sweet man," I replied. "But I want you to look at me very closely."

He studied my face, still drawing a blank.

"Do you remember a woman named Georgia who worked for your in-laws?"

"The name sounds vaguely familiar."

"She was my mom. She died a few years after your mother-in-law ran us out of the city."

"Why would she . . . ?" he began, and I could see the questions swirling in his head.

"Louis was my father, and Eliza knew it. She couldn't fire

my mother while he was alive, so she waited until the day of his funeral. Then she fired her and ruined her name. My mother couldn't find any more work in Philadelphia, so we had to leave. Your wife is my half-sister," I reported, smiling.

"Oh, my god," he said, sobering up as he put his hand to his head in disbelief.

"It's okay, though. No need to worry. Our secret's safe."

"Why would you—"

"Don't worry, Thomas. But again, our secret is safe," I said, heading for the door.

As I opened it the big surprise was when he called to me from the bed, saying, "Give me a call next week."

I laughed, shaking my wet mane behind me as I strutted out the door and headed to Camden to meet my man.

That night I made up with Ishmael in a big way, and I fell asleep with a smile of satisfaction on my face and, surprisingly, not a bit of guilt on my conscience.

16

One of the things that Ishmael and I did on Sunday after church and brunch was to go for a drive. It was a holdover from my time in Atlanta, when I first began plotting the lifestyle that I'd be able to afford when I "made it big." It was an innocent thing, but it was also something that gave me hope. Even now, sitting on a pile of money, I still enjoyed looking at grand houses because grand houses gave me hope, and I wanted to share a part of that hope with Ishmael.

So after leaving Center City restaurant one Sunday, he suggested going somewhere other than the opulent neighborhoods where we typically ventured in our explorations.

"What do you have in mind?"

"I don't know. You know the city better than I do."

"Let's drive past my properties."

"They're all over the city. That could take hours."

"Well, there's East Falls."

"That's near your place. I've already seen that on my way to see you."

"Chestnut Hill?" I suggested.

"It's pretty, eclectic, but we've toured it."

"West Mt. Airy?"

"Nice, diverse, but been there, done that."

"I'm not sure what else there is to see," I said, out of ideas.

"What's that neighborhood near where you grew up? Where your mom worked?"

"East Oak Lane."

"Yeah. Let's go see that."

"Ish, it's hardly worth the trip. It's not a very large area, just a few blocks."

"That's okay. When we finish, we can go back to your place," he suggested, smiling mischievously.

I had no desire to drive through East Oak Lane. I hadn't been back since the night I'd driven there to confront Eliza about her getting rid of my properties. I didn't know how to explain that to Ishmael and not sound silly. After all, as he liked to say, he was "just a brother from the hood who was trying to make good." Inheritance and birthright were things that he never dreamed about, yet here I was, angry that mine had been sold out from under me; he would think that I should just be happy that someone had left something to me. All that he and Isaac had inherited at their mother's passing was heartache.

"Okay," I acquiesced, sliding the car into drive and aiming toward Broad Street.

As we drove north, away from the congestion of downtown, I watched the neighborhoods change. The mayor had pumped millions of dollars into renovating the corridor that led to the chic theater, shopping, museum, and restaurant districts, which were all frequented by tourists and residents alike. After that, there was a bleak stretch of underdeveloped property, with liquor stores, nail salons, braiding shops, pawnshops, and churches alternating in the dominant positions from block to block. Then we came to Temple University, where the sidewalks were swept clean and the blindingly bright stadium lights overhead assured parents that their children would not be gobbled up by North Philly. After Temple was another expanse of urban wasteland, with prostitutes and addicts lurking in the shadows of abandoned factories; looking at the abandoned Botany 500 clothing factory, I was struck by the building's residential potential.

"Look at that," I said. "The structure of that is amazing."

Ishmael leaned over to get a better view. "You're right. They don't make them like that anymore. How many years has it been empty?"

"I'm not sure. It seems like it's been vacant most of my life, but my mother said that my father used to wear Botany 500 coats," I added quietly.

"Must have been pretty good quality stuff," he asserted. "The light's green."

I was lifting my foot from the brake and beginning to pull off when a shopping cart filled with junk drifted into my view.

"Watch out!" Ishmael called.

I slammed on the brakes, but not before toppling the cart. Its owner, an old lady garbed in layers of filthy rags, screamed streams of obscenities at me while hitting the hood of my car with her hand.

"Stay here," Ishmael said, hopping out of the car.

He rushed over to the woman with his hands raised slightly in a show of surrender. I rolled the window down and heard him ask her if she was okay.

She gesticulated wildly, pointing at me and then pointing down at her shopping cart. Words poured out of her mouth as Ishmael tried to quiet her.

I jumped out of the car. "Ma'am, I'm sorry. Let me help you with your things."

I bent toward the shopping cart, and Ishmael followed my lead, setting it upright as I began piling her belongings back inside.

"Hey, be careful with that," she ordered.

I apologized again and continued retrieving the things that lay in a heap before me. Silk sweaters, grubby from lack of care. A pair of badly worn Burberry slacks. Mikasa plates. What was this bummy old woman doing with these things?

When all her belongings were back in her cart, I walked over to the car for my purse while Ishmael tried to pacify the woman.

Her voice drifted over to me as I pulled a handful of bills out of my wallet. ". . . It ain't no Mercedes like hers, but it's all I got now. She don't know what it's like. She could end up just like me. Driving like she's crazy without regard for everyday folks," she continued as I approached her.

"Ma'am, I'm really sorry about your cart. The light was green, and I didn't see you. Here," I said, extending my hand with five fifty-dollar bills in it.

She stopped complaining and reached for the money. As I handed over the bills I looked into her face. I could tell that in her day she'd been beautiful. Now, lines creased her face, and her missing teeth made a checkerboard smile as she flipped through the bills. I felt bad for the homeless woman because I knew what it was like to be displaced and to not have a real place to call home.

"Ma'am, I'm going to give you my number. I have a place where you could stay," I offered.

"I don't need nothin' from you . . . but a few more of these," she said, fingering the crisp bills with her thin fingers, each with a long, ragged nail.

I retrieved a few more bills from my wallet and handed them to her, apologizing again. She stuffed the bills into her brassiere and started off again, back straight and shoulders squared with one foot in front of the other, her rickety cart in tow.

"Wow!" I said, settling back into the car. "I didn't even see her."

"Don't worry. I don't think she'll be back to haunt you."

"I know, but . . ."

"What?" he asked.

"Did you see the things in her cart?"

"Not really. I didn't examine them. I was just trying to get her stuff out of the street."

"She had some pretty high-end things in there."

"She probably found them."

"Maybe," I continued, not really believing it. Despite the coarseness of her speech and appearance, her bearing said that she had once held a much higher station in life. But how could someone who had been high fall low? I wondered as I tried to shake myself back to the present. It was true that my and my mother's fortunes had taken a turn for the worse after my father died, but in actuality, our fall hadn't been as tragic as this woman's seemed to have been.

"You know, I don't feel much like cruising anymore," I said.

189

"Yeah, I know what you mean," Ishmael replied, looking at his watch.

"I just want to go home and relax in the tub."

We drove back to Camden in relative silence with Freddie Hubbard's trumpet wafting over us, but it did nothing to soothe my soul as it usually did.

When I got home, I sat in my office at the computer, piecing together a story to submit for the gossip column.

The lights of A.C. twinkled a little brighter over the weekend as a few high-profile visitors alighted on the city by the sea. R & B crooner Joelle, who was featured in a recent issue of a celebrity magazine renewing his vows with his wife, was spotted with his arm draped around a blond who didn't resemble his Ethiopian bride one bit.

News anchor Peach Harrison was spotted getting onboard the yacht of sports agent Ted Bancroft along with football stars Bailey Reynolds and Phantom Holman. Word on the street is that Holman has become fond of recreational substances of the powdery sort. Since news like that rarely stays undercover for long, more is sure to unfold on that story.

On a different front, the Philadelphia-born model Minka will be featured in a fashion spread in the November issue of Elle magazine. The model has been linked with a popular New York DJ, and he is said to have helped show her around the NY party scene, where she met some of the players in the industry.

I'll be back next week with more juicy news and hot gossip about Philly and beyond.

The Social Butterfly

I e-mailed a copy of the article to Suzanne, and then I took a copy of it with me to my bedroom, where I sat on the bed rereading it. Though it had been composed very hurriedly, I hadn't done a bad job of it. This new gig wasn't something that I put a lot of stock into. Although I'd been socializing in this great city since I'd returned, now I was getting a chance to do it on the other side of the serving table where I'd been relegated in my past life.

If Ishmael's response to accompanying me to these events would be the same as it had been to attending the Bancrofts' boat christening, I'd be free to mingle and get story ideas. It wasn't that he didn't enjoy socializing. It was just that he had to do so much of it for fund-raising purposes that he preferred to keep things low-key in his downtime. I respected that, but there would be times when he'd have to compromise, I thought, as I lay the article on my nightstand and walked into the bathroom, where I sat on the edge of the tub, checking the warm water that I'd been running.

As I sank into the tub the weekend's events floated through my mind, and my thoughts were drawn back to the woman I'd almost hit that afternoon. Again I wondered what had happened to her to bring her so low.

"She could end up just like me." Her words echoed in my head as I dried off and slathered on moisturizer.

I settled into bed, and the last thought that I remembered having was that the high could always be made low. A name flashed through my mind as I plunged into sleep.

17

The next morning I sat in a staff meeting, discussing Sweeps Week in May. Ours was already the most popular station in the region for morning and nightly news, but the general manager wanted to make sure that we kept our lead. As he discussed strategy my mind wandered, and I remembered the idea that had come to me last night.

Eliza Harrison had been only mildly embarrassed by her outlandish interview on *Around Philly*. Her faux pas could be chalked up to her age, and she'd been taken back into the fold, though kept at arm's length. I wanted something more damaging. I wanted her to know how I had felt during childhood. Displaced, insecure, vulnerable. A perfect way to do that was to displace her. Let her know what it was like to not have a home. But how? I was turning the question over in my mind when Diana Davis, my producer, nudged me.

"All week she'll be doing guest spots on all our shows, the Sunday talk show, the morning news, *Around Philly*, *News at Noon*, the evening news, and *Friday Night Lights*. They'll all be leading up to the big night, on Saturday's nightly news."

"Who's he talking about?" I whispered to Diana.

She scribbled a name: Bridget Boudoir.

"That can't be her real name," I whispered, laughing.

"It might as well be. You don't know who she is?"

I shrugged.

"I'll tell you later," she said, and we turned our attention back to the meeting.

"Ratings are going to soar. In the meantime, keep up the good work. Have a good week."

I waited for Diana as she gathered her notepad and her coffee mug.

"So who is she?" I asked as we walked down the hallway toward the set.

"She's this reporter who is known for pushing the envelope. She used to be known for wearing clothes that were, let's say, less than professional. But then she just lost her mind and reported the news in the buff one night during Sweeps."

"You're kidding," I declared, dumbfounded.

"Nope. The station, I think it was in Florida, got a lot of flak about it, since it was regular television, not cable. But since it was after eleven o'clock, the decency laws didn't quite pertain, or something like that."

"That's crazy," I said, walking to the set.

"Sex sells."

"I know it." I, too, had pushed the envelope with some eye-popping attire, but integrity wouldn't let me give it away for free.

"Well, anyway, she's making a killing going from city to city doing guest spots at different stations."

"I guess so. It's like a traveling porn show."

Diana laughed and I headed toward my mark, temporarily forgetting about Eliza Harrison. Bridget Boudoir was occupying my thoughts for the moment. She might gain a good deal of attention and money from sanctioned stripping post–prime time, but there was room for only one star at this station, and it wasn't her.

Ishmael and I sat at the bar of a new restaurant during its grand opening. I had received a hand-delivered invitation at the station, promising free drinks, appetizers, promo materials, and future meals if I attended the event. Other local celebs turned out, including a few of the 76ers, a local fashion designer who outfitted some A-list actresses, a rising star on the rap scene who had Philly roots, and a few young businessmen. This wasn't Ishmael's idea of a good time, but I talked him into coming by convincing him of the networking benefits for Camden Academy. With that as a carrot, he gladly accepted.

On the way there, he mock-complained, saying, "I don't know how I ended up with someone who likes to go out so much."

"It takes somebody like me to pull you off of the couch."

"I put in a lot of hours, and when I'm not working, I just like to relax."

"I understand. Just as long as you come out with me to social events every once in a while."

The funny thing was, after we walked past the velvet rope holding back the line of people waiting to get in, he saw some of the ballplayers and perked right up. I made the rounds, mingling with people, but when I checked in with Ish periodically, I heard him talking about mentoring his students and getting donations for next year's auction. Whether he admitted it or not, he was in his element, and I joked with him about it as we sat at the bar, eating a scrumptious strawberry-ginger chicken appetizer.

"From the way you were talking, you were going to be sitting in the corner sulking and nursing the same drink all night," I gibed.

"Well, every now and then it's good to mix things up and meet new people."

"I'm glad you came around. Ooh, I almost forgot. Speaking of new people, the station is bringing in a guest reporter for Sweeps week."

"Anybody I know?"

"I hope not. Her name is Bridget Boudoir, and . . ."

"Are you serious?"

"Why, do you know her?"

"Just of her. She's like a stripper with a microphone," he said, grinning.

"Oh, you know her fine journalistic work, I see."

He laughed. "She can't hold a candle to you."

"I'm sure. Just don't let me catch you hanging around the station during the week that she's here," I said, giving him a swat with pseudo-jealousy in my voice.

I got up and headed toward the ladies' room, returning people's greetings and acknowledgments along the way.

I was smoothing my clothing inside the spacious stall when I heard the bathroom door open and low voices speaking.

"I can't believe she has the nerve to sit perched at that bar like she's the belle of the damn ball. They may not know who she really is, but to me she'll always be the maid's bastard daughter."

"Elicia, it's not that serious."

"She shouldn't have embarrassed our grandmother on television like that, holding her up for everyone to ridicule."

"Grandmother did that to herself. She shouldn't have gone on that show anyway, because you know how folks view organizations like that. They think we're elitist and everything else without seeing the good side. Besides that, grandmother is old and forgetful, and she's bound to say or do just about anything. Anyway, that was months ago, so just drop it. Fix your face, and let's go. Your husband and my fiancé are waiting for us."

I peeked out of the crack in the stall to get a glimpse of the two cousins, my nieces, who had obviously inherited their mothers' dispositions. We were all roughly the same age, as Momma had been pregnant with me at the same time that Elizabeth and Louise had been expecting. I could see only the back of one, but I memorized every pattern in that silver brocade sheath so that I could zero in on her when I got back to the bar.

When I was sure that they'd gone, I emerged from the stall and looked at myself. I hadn't noticed the lump in my throat as I'd overheard them talking, but as I studied my reflection I saw my eyebrows furrow and felt myself tearing up. I forestalled a breakdown by giving myself an internal slap. Yes, my mother had been a maid, but that wasn't the only thing that she was. She was a designer and a seamstress extraordinaire. She was also their grandfather's mistress, so if they insisted on acting ugly, then so would I.

I made my way back to Ishmael's side and kissed him on the cheek. I scanned the room, looking for Elicia and her cousin Lindsay until I spotted them. Wearing that silver brocade sheath, Elicia, who had grown plump over the years, looked like a baked potato. Her thick brown hair was cut in spiky layers that made her look like a porcupine.

Next to her stood a caramel-colored man with a strong, square jaw and almond-shaped eyes. His mouth broke into a smile in response to what someone else in his party said. As he laughed he threw back his head, and as he resumed his conversation his eyes locked with mine.

"This should be easy," I almost said aloud.

Ishmael stood up for round two of his social swirl. "I'm going to talk to a few more folks, and then I'll be ready whenever you are."

"Okay," I replied, taking a sip of the cranberry juice in front of me on the bar.

The woman next to me struck up a conversation about the interview that I'd done with Patti LaBelle the week before when she was promoting her new cookbook. We'd talked as we made our way around the set kitchen, whipping up a Sunday brunch whose flavor matched the singer's vocal acrobatics.

"I'm glad that you enjoyed the interview. The food really was good," I said.

"I know. I've heard that she can throw down. I feel silly asking you this, but where did you get the white blouse you wore that day?"

I racked my brain, trying to remember what I'd worn. As

I was thinking, a male voice said, "I hate to interrupt, but I wanted to get your autograph before I go."

I turned around and found myself eye to eye with Elicia's husband. I smiled brightly with a hint of seduction in my eyes as he grinned in return.

"Sure, sir." I said. "Where should I sign?"

Pushing a business card toward me, he said, "Anywhere you want."

I lowered my eyes and peeked up through my lashes, as I'd seen Miss Mamie do numerous times years before.

"I'm Nelson Skinner."

"Peach Harrison. Nice to meet you."

"The pleasure's all mine. Do you have a card? Maybe we can have lunch and talk about your assets."

A glance at his business card told me that he was an investment banker.

"Why? Could you help me improve them?"

"They look just fine to me, but maybe a closer inspection is in order."

"Maybe."

I was quiet then. Without looking, I knew that the woman to my right was listening to every word passing between us.

"You can reach me at the station if you choose," I said. I had already tangled with his father-in-law, who was still sniffing around the station, trying to get back in contact with me. I didn't need another of the clan in my life, even though it would feel good to get back at Elicia for her bitchiness.

"Okay. You have my number, too. Don't let it get lost."

"Okay," I replied, smiling.

As he moved away the woman next to me asked, "Is it like that all the time? Men throwing themselves at you? If so, I'm in the wrong business."

Laughing, I said, "I get to meet lots of interesting people."

"Interesting, nothing. That man is fine, but you'd better watch out for him."

"I'm already spoken for, but just out of curiosity, what do you know about him?"

"He doesn't remember me, but we went to high school together. He actually got put out in his senior year because of some scandal with his grades. They tried to keep it hush-hush, but they said it had something to do with changing his transcripts. His parents were pretty powerful, so they were able to make that go away, but it ruined any chance of his going to law school after college like he'd wanted to. He went into banking instead. He's doing pretty well, if I understand correctly, but he's always reaching for something new."

"What do you mean?"

"Let's just say he likes women—a lot of women. And he's not known for being good to them."

"What?"

"I work for the District Attorney's office so I really can't say more than that, but be careful."

"Interesting. I doubt that I'll ever speak to him again, but thanks for the warning."

"Anytime."

Stars alighted on Center City last night at the opening of Crayons, a new hot spot nestled into cozy Olde City. It was wall-to-wall power-brokers, with rising young professionals

*like hot ad exec Melinda Luster, public relations maven
Bibi Hampton, and entertainment attorney Leslie Garrison.
Also in the mix were 76ers teammates Elmer McWhorter,
Doug Clark, and Tommy Settles. Married investment
banker Nelson Skinner was seen lingering very near a
media personality, which might spell trouble for his wife,
considering the rumors about how his roving eye and
hands almost got him in legal trouble not long ago. It seems
that he was entertaining three, um, let's say, dancers, in
his secret hideaway, and things got a little too exotic. The
trouble, however, was swept away easily.*

*Rapper Louton disappeared with an unidentified fan
and reappeared smiling and disheveled. I certainly hope
that he suited up before taking the dive, because he's
already got six mouths to feed, including one that's just
two months old.*

*Do you remember when I told you about Phantom
Holman's dabbling in powdery substances? Well, his
team's spokesman is set to issue a statement next week that
Holman's checking into an Arizona treatment center. No
word about whether he'll get the ax from the team. As soon
as I know, though, you'll know.*

*I'll be back next week with more juicy news and hot
gossip about Philly and beyond.*

Satisfied, I reread the article before e-mailing it to Suzanne. The allusion to Nelson Skinner's wandering eye was
especially pleasing to me, considering how his wife had
bad-mouthed me in the bathroom. Serves that fat bitch right.
Maybe this would give her something to think about the
next time she wanted to malign someone.

18

Bridget Boudoir blew into Philadelphia in the late spring like a storm, dripping diamonds and oozing sensuality. She was flamboyant, fierce, and free. She spoke her mind, and she was unapologetic about what she said. In her brief stay here, she went from being my worst nightmare, because of the potential career threat that she posed, to being my hero, because of her take-what-you-want attitude.

Bob Trent, the general manager, welcomed her by opening his home to us all on Saturday for a cocktail party. She showed up late, flirted with a sexy young server, paid little attention to us, and left with the young man on her arm. We were left standing in the aura of her perfume, scratching our heads and wondering if she'd show up in time for the first show she had to do on Sunday.

Angry and disappointed, the GM mumbled, "For a hundred thousand dollars, she'd better be early and have a smile on her face." Then he threw back his head and downed his martini.

Sunday found me curious and alert, sitting in front of the television as I got dressed for church services with Ishmael. I was wondering if she'd deliver. So many times I'd seen people only amount to fool's gold when they'd touted themselves as the Real McCoy. She was the latter—and more—as she sat in on the local political roundtable show. Wearing a stylish though Victorian high-collared blouse with a salmon silk pantsuit and conservative matching pumps, she asked pointed questions as if she'd lived in Philly her entire life and followed politics with a fervor.

On Monday, when she showed up for the morning news, I eyed her as she approached the set, wearing a lavender silk skirt suit with a conservative blouse that was less demure than Sunday's. Her delivery was flawless, her diction was perfect, and her smiles were dazzling. I was as awed as the men on the set were. Yet for all of her professionalism, she made no attempt to talk to me during breaks.

On Tuesday she joined me on *Around Philly*, wearing a teal suit with a simple shell underneath. Her shoes, though high-heeled and a lot flashier than Monday's, were still tasteful and elegant. We played off each other, and after the show ended, she acknowledged me with a smile and a wink before putting her omnipresent shades back on.

On Wednesday Bridget joined me for *News at Noon*, and her hair, which had begun the week in an austere bun before moving into a loose ponytail and then a flat-ironed pageboy look, was a mass of fluffy, fun curls. She wore a soft gray swing jacket, a lacy smoke-colored shell, and a slim soft gray skirt that was considerably higher than yesterday's.

And the shoes, which were more for the crew, producer, and on-air personalities, were sexy, strappy sandals that showed off beautiful, pampered feet. After the show, she looked me in the eye, leaned over to me, and said, "I can see the star in you. Don't sit around waiting for it to come to you. Do it to death, damn it."

Before I could ask her what "it" was, she replaced her shades and floated off in a cloud of perfume.

On Thursday she was a part of the evening news team, and in keeping with the foreplay that her previous appearances had been, she wore less, garbing herself in a thin, floating crimson chiffon dress. Her curls were tousled in a sexy, morning-after look.

I wanted to see her face-to-face again to ask what she had meant by her comment. Actually, I think I already knew, but I was looking for clarification and inspiration. Ishmael was a cheerleader for me, applauding me for the accolades that came my way from local civic organizations, and Miss Mamie always congratulated me on the good news that I shared with her, but for some reason I was looking for more. To date, I had been driven by revenge, which had been good enough motivation for me, but when that waned, what would be left? I tried seeking Bridget out. I called her at her hotel, but she didn't return my call, and I was left looking for a sign.

Friday found her on *Friday Night Lights*, a sports show hosted by an ex–football player turned reporter. He could barely keep his tongue in his mouth as he regarded her in her sleeveless, body-skimming chocolate sheath with the split up to there and the neckline down to there. Nonetheless, she remained professional as always as she discussed both local and national sports with authority. When the show ended, viewers across the Delaware Valley sat blinking at their television screens, wondering what the next night would bring.

I invited Ishmael over on Saturday to watch the nightly news, and as we nestled on the loveseat in the sitting area of my bedroom he asked me if I'd had the opportunity to talk to her at all.

"Not really. She was a little aloof to all of us at the station, but she did give me a little advice."

"About what?"

"My career."

"What did she say?"

"She just told me to go ahead and take it to the next level."

"What does that mean?"

"Do a national show."

"I never knew that's what you wanted."

"Ever since I was a little girl," I replied, smiling a small smile.

"Did she give you any tips?"

"Sort of."

His mouth was open, poised to ask me a question, when the news started. Then he forgot what he was going to say.

"I sure hope that you're this attentive when I'm on," I said with mock sarcasm.

He just smiled, watching the show's introduction.

The news went as expected, and, as we would learn at the end of Sweeps, our ratings were through the roof. But that night, after the news ended, I made passionate love to Ishmael, all the while thinking of shooting stars.

19

"It's good hearing from you," Thomas Brooks said, the smile in his voice evident.

"I've been thinking about you, and I wanted to reach out," I responded.

"Thanks. I didn't know what to think after that night in Atlantic City."

"Why think anything? We were just having fun."

"I know that, but technically you're my sister-in-law."

"Your wife would never admit that, so neither will I."

"So what is this about?"

"I told you, baby, it's about fun," I said. Although I'd never verbalize it, revenge was definitely key in the equation.

"Okay," he said, pausing. "So when can we have fun again?"

"Whenever you want."

"How about today? I don't have another client until two-thirty."

"Aren't you the eager one?" I teased.

"It's been awhile."

"Let's say tomorrow right after I sign off from *News at Noon*. Where can we meet?"

"I have an apartment in Center City."

"Why's that?"

"Late nights in the office. Sometimes early court dates. I hate having to trek all the way to the suburban hell where she insisted on buying a house in a gated community."

"Oh," I replied, only half listening as I queued up the tape I was about to watch.

"So, one o'clock at the Dorchester."

"Sounds fine."

"The doorman will buzz you up."

"Okay. See you then," I said, smiling salaciously.

In the weeks after Bridget left, I brainstormed and searched through archives of my show, attempting to find my best interviews and hottest segments. I was pulling them together for an audition tape that I was submitting to Walter Sirianni, the network executive in charge of new-show development. Philadelphia was a great market, and most of the television personalities had longevity, so my future was becoming more secure the longer I stayed. What I really wanted, however, was to kick my game way up and go national. I shared that thought with Thomas when I met him at his apartment that afternoon.

"Do it. You'd be great at it. I like your current show."

"Thanks," I replied, wrapped in a silk sheet on the bed.

"Let me know when the draft of your contract comes in. I'll look it over for you."

"Thanks. You're such a sweet man. Too bad your woman doesn't appreciate you."

A look of sadness washed across his face before he turned to the glass of dark rum on his nightstand. He tossed his head back and downed the drink in one gulp.

"It's okay. I appreciate you," I asserted, standing to retrieve my purse from the wingback chair on the other side of the room. "That's why I got you this."

I presented him with a small jewelry box. He opened it and smiled.

"What's this? White gold?" he asked, examining the cuff links in the black velvet box.

"Platinum. I had them designed especially for you," I said, smiling. I'd visited a jeweler I'd met and talked him through the design that I wanted. A peach diamond in a rectangular setting with a Florentine finish. I'd purchased two sets of them, one for Thomas and one for Ishmael. In Ishmael's, instead of peach diamonds I'd had rubies, which symbolized my heart, set.

"That was sweet of you," Thomas said. "Come here and let me show you my appreciation."

I walked back to the bed, where he wrapped his arms around me and kissed me passionately. Then he rolled me onto my back while his tongue made a line down my neck, between my breasts and down my stomach.

The early November wind whipped past me as I returned to the station after my romp with Thomas, and I called the network's headquarters in New York. I'd set up an appointment with Walter Sirianni, and I was calling his secretary to get the inside scoop on some of his preferences. From sports to candy, I was out to woo him to get what I wanted. Some might consider it payola, but I knew that it was done all the time. By the end of the week, I'd put together a basket that included floor seats to a 76ers game, gift cards for the Georgette Klinger spa, truffles from a Swiss chocolatier, and a box of my favorite white-flesh doughnut peaches. It was hand-delivered by a service specializing in personal touches, so the delivery woman, a leggy Latina garbed in a peach silk suit, arrived on Friday morning at eleven o'clock, saying, "Miss Peach Harrison looks forward to meeting with you on Wednesday."

She called me from the lobby and reported his response.

"He was beaming when I left."

"Great," I replied, hanging up the phone in my office, where I sat reviewing the tape again. I had just come off the set, and I was pulling together my package. I wanted to have it perfect before I left it alone for a few days, because I didn't want to be too wound up when Wednesday came.

The phone rang again, and I answered promptly.

"Peach Harrison."

"Hey, Claudia," Ishmael's soothing voice oozed.

"Hi, baby," I responded, settling back into my chair. "I'm glad you called. I'm a little tense about my meeting with Sirianni on Wednesday."

"You should be. It's a big move, but I don't think there's anyone more ready or capable."

I sat quietly, letting his words sink in. Next to Miss Mamie, he really was my biggest cheerleader. Although my actions didn't show it, I really did love him. Since the first time I saw him, he'd been the carrot swinging at the end of the line for me, the proverbial pot of gold at the end of a long whirl of colors. My life had been a swirl of dreary blues and upbeat skies, envious greens and soothing sages, raging reds and unruffled roses. The dreariness, envy, and rage had fueled me for so long, and, in truth, they had been as responsible for my success as my pure ambition. Now that I was on my way to where I wanted to be professionally and socially, I didn't want those same things to ruin me and my relationship with the man I loved. But my heart felt as if it was in a tug of war between passive peace that I could have with Ishmael and the satisfying retribution that I felt needed to be meted out.

Thomas was a pawn for me, just a piece in my game of revenge, and I was almost ready to be done with him. Ishmael, on the other hand, was the person I wanted in my life forever. I know that it didn't seem like it, with my preoccupation with revenge, but I kept hoping that once I'd gotten it out of my system, I'd be free of that baggage.

"Thanks. I'm glad that you're taking the day off from school and going with me."

"I wouldn't miss it. What time do you want me to come pick you up today?"

"Four. I'll meet you in the lobby."

"That's okay. I know how you pack. You'll never even make it to the elevator with all those bags, even though it's just a weekend trip to the Poconos."

Laughing, I said, "Alright. See you then. Love you."

"Love you, too."

Wednesday morning came, and I tried to still myself with pleasant, calming thoughts. I rarely got flustered before a meeting, but afterward my stomach was always in knots. As Ishmael and I rode the Amtrak train through New Jersey he talked about some of his students.

"If I wasn't a praying man when I started in education, I certainly am now."

"My mother used to say that when kids are little, they're under your feet, but when they grow up, they're on your mind. Or something like that."

"I guess I know what she meant by that. I've got this one kid who . . . ," he began, happily distracting me from the nerves that had gone haywire with anxiety about my meeting.

The meeting went better than I could have hoped. In the hour that I had with Walter Sirianni, I sold myself like a sinner trying to get through the pearly gates. I showed the five-minute sample of my work that precedes the rest of the clips I wanted to showcase. I talked about my target demographic, best possible times for the show to air, potential advertisers, promotional techniques, and sample show ideas. He smiled the entire time, closing out our meeting by saying that my ideas were intriguing, and that he was more than interested. Ishmael, who had been sitting in the waiting area, smiled broadly when he saw me.

"You're glowing," he said.

"Can't talk yet," I said through my plastered-on smile.

I made a beeline for the bathroom, where the butterflies fluttering in my stomach were unleashed in a hail of vomit.

"All better," I said, emerging from the ladies' room.

Rumor has it that fabulous Philadelphia television personality Peach Harrison is being considered for a new gig. Her show, Around Philly, *which highlights arts,* culture, events, and fun folks, could be broadened for a national audience beginning as early as the fall. The stylish news anchor and talk show host is remaining tight-lipped about the potential deal, but more news will surely follow.

Ricky Nesbitt, longtime wife of 76ers star Danny Nesbitt, is set to launch an upscale sportswear line. The line will be called Behind the Bench, and it will be featured first at Macy's stores throughout the Delaware Valley.

Larry Panera, president of Philadelphia Consolidated Energy Company, has got some explaining to do. It seems that he and his young mistress were spotted dawdling in a Manayunk maternity store last weekend while his wife was out of town. The would-be future Mrs. Panera tried on scores of outfits while her sugar daddy lounged in the waiting area, "camouflaged" by sunglasses and a baseball cap. It could be lights out for Larry's marriage.

That's the dish for now. I'll be back next week with more juicy news and hot gossip about Philly and beyond.

The Social Butterfly

20

"Yes, Miss Mamie, it really went well. Walter Sirianni, the network exec I met with, seemed really interested. He called me the next day and thanked me for coming in and for the gifts that I sent him."

"What else did he say?"

"He said that the Peach show could be a breath of fresh air, a change from the trashy talk shows that are flooding the airwaves now. He called me a hip, young Oprah."

"Well, girl, it sounds like you've got it made. You'll be ready to go before you know."

I laughed at her rhyme, which she probably did unconsciously at this point.

"I sure hope so," I said, reaching for the large pile of mail that had been accumulating over the past weeks. I had pulled the bills out of the pile and paid them immediately, but the catalogs and other stuff had grown into a mini mound. I flipped through it while Miss Mamie talked about the basket of shower gels and lotions that I had sent her.

"I'm glad you like them," I commented absently while my eyes came to rest on an ivory linen envelope. Turning it over, I saw the engraved return address on the back.

The Philadelphia Chapter. The Coterie, Incorporated. 525 Westview Lane. Philadelphia. What could that be? Probably another invitation to attend an event. I received tons of them in the mail at work, but rarely did I receive them at home.

"Mm-hmm," I agreed absently while Miss Mamie rattled along, talking about her favorite soap opera.

Slicing the envelope open, I saw that it was a letter signed by Louise Harrison Simpson and Evelyn Moore, cochairs of the Women to Watch Luncheon.

"Miss Mamie," I said, interrupting her. "You'll never believe who sent me a letter."

"Who?"

"Louise Harrison."

"What does she want?"

"I don't know. I haven't read it yet. Let me see."

Dear Ms. Harrison,

The Philadelphia Chapter of The Coterie, Inc., has honored some of the rising stars for the past two decades. Past honorees have included City Councilwoman Lydia Smithson before *she successfully ran for mayor, Zelda Walden* before *she was appointed to a federal judgeship,*

Danielle Kenner before *she took the helm of Computech,
and Van Blount* before *she was named chief medical officer
of Infinity Insurance. We saw their potential and drive
long before anyone else took notice. We see the same drive
in you.*

*We are well aware of your current position in the
Philadelphia media. You are respected and regarded highly
by viewers throughout the tristate area, and we see that
your star is poised to go even higher. We want you to take
an afternoon to enjoy your success, and we want to revel in
it with you.*

*With that in mind, we are extending an invitation to
you to join us for our annual luncheon, which will be held
at the Four Seasons on Sunday, May 1. We look forward to
your prompt response, and we wish you Godspeed in your
endeavors.*

> *Best wishes,*
> *Louise Harrison Simpson*
> *Evelyn Moore*
> *Cochairs*

Scrawled underneath was a handwritten note that
read, "Please be in touch. I have something that I believe
is yours."

"Ooh, child. That's good. People should give you your
flowers now while you're treading earth."

"Yeah, I suppose it is a nice honor. Other groups have honored me, too, but The Coterie is . . ."

"Big time. I know. Your momma and me always called 'em
hincty folks. I catered some of their shindigs when I was
living there. All those women, drippin' with jewels and

whatnot. Most of them were decent. Polite. A little standoff-ish, but I suppose we all can be that way. But a few of them were pistols. Didn't think it was right for us common folks to breathe the same air."

"Like Eliza Harrison."

"Especially Eliza Harrison."

"Well, what do you make of the fact that her daughter signed the letter?"

"Nothing and everything. Maybe she's acknowledging that this is a new day."

I was quiet for a few seconds, considering the possibilities.

"Suppose it's a trick?" I proposed, feeling vulnerable and small.

"I doubt it. What would they stand to gain from bringing you in there to trick you?"

"Maybe they want to finish the work Eliza started with Momma and ruin me permanently."

"Elizabeth is catty enough to try something like that, but if I recall, Louise was always decent."

I had to agree with that. She'd stuck up for me as a kid when Elizabeth had tried to berate me for the speech I delivered at St. Luke's. Come to think of it, she'd always been at least cordial to me, as if she'd recognized my humanity when the rest of her family hadn't.

"You are going to attend, aren't you?"

As I turned the issue over in my mind I decided right then.

"What have I got to lose?"

That night I wrote my acceptance letter on the Mrs. John L. Strong stationery that I reserved for special occasions, and I set it on the nightstand next to Momma's picture. As I nestled into my bed preparing for sleep to wash over me, a lone tear slid out of my eye. It was a tear of happiness at the public acknowledgment, the familial acceptance that I'd craved all my life and was finally getting. Drifting off to sleep, I dreamed a happy dream about Momma.

21

The cold, gray days of winter were like wet wool, which refuses to do anything but sop and stink, and I grew anxious about the prospects of my national show. I started to call Walter half a dozen times, but I decided against it. From scribbling a thank-you-for-the-meeting-and-potential-opportunity note to sending him another box of doughnut peaches, I'd done everything I could think of to keep myself in the foreground of his mind. The ball was now in his court, and I had to wait it out. To ease the excruciating passage of time, I decided to throw a "Beat the Blahs" party.

I flew Miss Mamie up to Philly, where she stayed with me, and invited some of the folks from the station, members of my sorority whom I'd gotten to know over the years, and some folks from the social scene who were good people. Ishmael brought Isaac, who, in turn, brought one of his incredibly beautiful but awfully shallow dates to adorn his arm. I rented out a spa in Center City that had opened just a few months before. They were thankful for the business, and they let us have the run of the place. After the spa treatments, we trickled little by little over to the Indian restaurant next door, then concluded the evening with dancing at a Latin club on Delaware Avenue, the city's up-and-coming club district on the Delaware River.

When Miss Mamie and I dragged ourselves home on the cusp of dawn, there was one message on the answering machine in my room. As I listened to it, an unfamiliar voice spoke: "This message is for Peach Harrison. This is Walter Sirianni. Formal acknowledgment is coming soon, but I wanted to be the first to tell you that we have some planning to do. Looking forward to speaking with you. Bye."

"Woo!" I screamed, rushing toward Miss Mamie, who was sitting on my bed. I threw my arms around her, gushing, "The Peach show is a go!"

"Congratulations, baby!" she gushed, pressing me as close to her as she could. "Congratulations, child!"

The next few weeks were a flurry of activity as I jetted back and forth between New York and Philadelphia, making plans for shooting a few pilot episodes. Thomas had been helpful enough to look over the paperwork for me, and every now and then I rewarded him right there in his office.

Despite his professional success and financial comfort, I actually felt pity for him. He was such an unhappy man, and when he'd married Elizabeth Harrison, he hadn't known what he was signing up for. Marrying her had been the biggest mistake of his life. He'd told me that once as we talked over lunch at his Center City apartment, and he'd repeated that sentiment a dozen times since.

He told me how she berated him, constantly reminding him that he'd married up when they'd tied the knot. He told me how she'd curse him out without ever raising her icy voice, telling him he was lucky that she ever looked his way. He told me how for years she made him request sex in advance, and that he always had to perform oral sex on her first before she'd let him lay a finger on her. Even when she did give her body to him, it was grudgingly and passively, as if it were a chore she detested doing.

So he stopped asking.

And she never knew why. She assumed that it was another woman, so she worried. She, Elizabeth Harrison Brooks, could not lose her husband and become a single woman. Someone like her was supposed to be revered and doted on by everyone, especially her husband, so to retain or regain her position in his life, she cut off her unmarried friends, lost weight, and offered to go to counseling. Anything to maintain her image as the powerful attorney's wife.

"The irony of it," Thomas admitted as we lay on the plush bed of a Center City hotel, "was that there were no other women. I was celibate. A celibate married man. A celibate married man who had to drink in order to stomach her presence. But then you came along."

Our rendezvous weren't intensely passionate meetings. Often I simply sat and listened to him talk, which, he said, was something that his wife never made time to do, with all her social commitments. But we did have sex, too. It wasn't like the depths-of-my-soul-stirring, fiery interludes that I enjoyed with Ishmael, but it was simply a release, and I loved the idea that I was the one giving comfort to Elizabeth Harrison's husband. That had been revenge enough for me . . . until the note from Louise. Now I felt oddly optimistic about the new life I was going to begin, with me feeling like their emotional equals.

Yet, still, the affair had to end. I was thinking of how I'd sever my ties with him when the phone rang again.

"Peach Harrison," I answered.

"Hi, Peach. This is Louise Harrison Simpson. How are you?"

"Fine. Great. Thanks for returning my call," I said a bit stiffly, unsure of why she had instructed me to call her.

"Thanks for making the call. This is actually something that we should speak about face-to-face, but I think that you've waited long enough."

"Okay," I said, unsure of what she meant.

"I know that you're my half sister. We've all known for years, though not as long as our mother. When our father was in the hospital right before he died, our mother had power of attorney. When she knew how gravely ill he was, she got her hands on his will. Apparently, our father made provisions for your mother in the will," she said, pausing.

"What!" I shrieked, thinking of the way that Momma and I had struggled in Moultrie. If there had been money, maybe she could have paid for the medical attention she needed.

"I know that this is a shock, and I'm sure that there were times when that money would have come in handy when you left Philadelphia. I don't know how to repay you for that time."

"There's no way . . . ," I began, then stopped myself. She

wasn't trying to be the bearer of bad news. Nor was she trying to make me less angry about the past. She was simply explaining, so I let her.

"It turns out that your interview with Mother sparked a lot of debate in our family. Once she knew who you were, she told us, and a lot of old hurt came out. She told us about how you represented a lot of hurt for her, and how she treated you as a result of that. I'm really very sorry about that," she said, pausing again.

I couldn't respond. The tears that were spilling out of my eyes were also squeezing my throat closed.

"Anyway, the only way that we can partially make up for the past is to give you the money that our father intended Georgia to have when he died twelve years ago. We've added interest and an additional sum for the properties that you lost because of Mother's actions. I'd like to give this to you in person, if possible."

"Okay," I whimpered in a quiet voice.

"You've waited long enough. Are you available this afternoon?"

"Yes," I replied, still not trusting my voice to say anything more than that.

"I'll meet you at the family house in East Oak Lane at four."

"Okay."

That afternoon I sat in front of the Harrison house mustering the courage to get out of the car and walk to the front door. The last time I had been here was years ago on the night I was going to confront Eliza about getting rid of my property. Now here I was, about to get payment for my loss. As I opened the car door I wondered if there was ever enough money to erase hurt.

I climbed the front steps, feeling like I was shrinking with every step that I took toward the majestic house of torture. Louise opened the door smiling, and she embraced me warmly.

"I'm glad you could come."

"So am I," I said, stepping inside and surveying the familiar foyer. Not much had changed.

"Come into the living room," she said. "Mother isn't ready to face you, and Elizabeth couldn't be here, so it's just us. Is that okay?" she asked, as if there was anything I could do about it. Truthfully, the day had been such a shock to me that I wasn't sure if I could have handled seeing the other two today.

"Well, I don't have anything to say except I'm sorry for anything that I may have done to make you unhappy."

"No, you were always decent and kind to me," I said, reassuring her.

Louise smiled. "Mother says that's one thing that I have in common with Dad. Aside from being hurt by Dad's relationship with your mother, she was pretty embarrassed. She told me that she wanted to fire your mother, but Dad wouldn't hear of it. He said that would be indecent."

As Louise spoke I actually recalled that conversation, which I had overheard. I'd been about to enter his study with the latest editions of his favorite magazines when I'd heard Eliza's voice, sounding like I'd never heard it before. She'd seemed both angry and sad, vicious and pleading, and I didn't fully understand the context of the conversation until much later.

"How can you continue to employ her?" she'd asked, almost whining.

"She's a good worker, Eliza."

"She's a home wrecker," Eliza had hissed, and I thought about the plate that Momma had dropped that morning. Maybe she'd broken too many plates, and that's why Mrs. Harrison had said she wrecked her home.

"Do you know how you're humiliating me by continuing to employ her? Do you know how it makes me look when she shows up here every day, smiling, and bringing your . . . that . . . child with her? She's laughing at me."

"Georgia doesn't have that in her. She's a good person. She's a kid. I'm the one who's done wrong, and I know that I'll have to answer for it one day. But you won't make her pay for my mistake. You won't fire her. That would be indecent," he'd said with finality.

I'd heard something crash to the floor before seeing Eliza come rushing out of the room. Her face looked red and crumpled as if she might cry, but she didn't. At least not that I saw, but I knew that her words were angry.

Now Louise asked, "Is there anything that you'd like to get off your chest or that you want me to convey to Mother and Elizabeth?"

I thought about the affair that I'd been carrying on with Thomas, and for the first time I felt a tinge of guilt. I knew then that I'd had my last interlude with him.

"Not really. I suppose the apology could go both ways."

She looked at me sympathetically, probably thinking that I was apologizing for the television interview.

"Don't think of this money as a payoff or guilt money. Think of it as inclusion. Finally," she said, handing me a check for $400,000.

For me, money didn't have the power to truly assuage the pain of all of those years, because I couldn't be bought. But it was a start at making things a little better, and I would use the money to provide scholarships to graduating high school seniors who were interested in attending school and majoring in, what else, fashion design.

"So what are you going to buy me with all that money that's falling in your lap?" Ishmael teased as he sat across from me at the Chart House, a beautiful restaurant that overlooked the Delaware River, which separated Philly from Camden.

"I'm going to give away scholarships in Momma's name, and I was thinking about another piece of real estate. How about if I buy us a place in the Poconos? I can tape the show in New York, and you can run a mentoring program in North Jersey," I proposed. I was being serious, hoping that he would take the bait and consider the move.

"How about buying a place there that we can go to on weekends?" he suggested.

"Why make it a weekend place?" I asked. "You know, neither of us knows anybody up there, so it could be like we're starting over fresh."

He paused a moment before saying, "I like the people I already know, and I love my work. Besides, I could never leave Camden. What's all this talk about starting over someplace?"

"I don't know. I was just thinking about making a new start of everything."

"Oh," he said, considering my words. "Isaac and I made a promise to stay in Camden and work as long as we're effective. It's what we've got to do."

"Oh." I was defeated. Trying to hide my disappointment, I feigned perkiness. "It's no big deal. Just wanderlust, maybe. I'll get over it."

I had hoped that he'd take the plunge and want to leave. It wasn't a pressing desire but a thought. New job, new city. The commute could be made, but a place closer to work would be great. Of course, I could always get a small place near work while maintaining my place in Philly. Yet, if I was going to remain here for the long haul, and if things with Ishmael were going to be kicked up to the next level, I needed to take care of things with Thomas, and I hoped that doing so would soothe the uneasiness that had begun to gnaw at my gut.

22

"Well, Peach, you've got yourself a good deal," Thomas said, sitting back and smiling at me across the desk in his office. "You're going to be a rich woman."

While that was good news, it was far from the consolation that I needed to assuage the nervousness I was feeling. I couldn't understand where it was coming from or why now, when it looked as if my life was finally taking shape the way I wanted it to. Whatever it was had me filled with an unsettling queasiness that wouldn't leave.

Thomas wrapped up his explanation of the proposal by saying, "When the actual contract comes in, bring it in so that I can look it over. You shouldn't have any trouble with signing it, though. Even if the show doesn't air for some reason, you'll get fifty percent of the contract, which is still pretty sizable."

I'd had so many numbers thrown at me in the past few days that I could only get mildly excited. Besides, something more was weighing on me at the moment.

Although I had practiced the words I would use to sever our relationship, I smiled uncomfortably as I tried to will them to come out.

"What?" he asked, sensing my discomfort.

"I guess there's no way to say it but to say it," I mumbled.

His smiling face turned serious, and he cleared his throat. "I knew the day would come. You're young and beautiful, and you've got your whole life ahead of you. I shouldn't have gotten you involved in the first place. But, being selfish, I did."

"I was just as willing," I started, relieved that he was being gracious and letting me off the hook.

"I need to work things out with Elizabeth, and I'm going to need to really focus on it, because you know about all of the difficulties I've had with her," he said, reaching across the desk for my hands, which were on my lap.

I reciprocated. "You're a sweet man. Thank you for everything that you've taught me about what not to do in a marriage."

He kissed my fingers. "Good-bye, Peach," he said softly.

I stood with him still holding my hands.

"Good-bye, Thomas."

"I'll probably see you in a few weeks at The Coterie luncheon," he said as he moved around the desk, walking me toward the door. "And I'll still look over the final contract for you when it comes in."

"I appreciate that," I remarked quietly, sincerely grateful for his kindness.

He hugged me and kissed my forehead, and I walked out the door with my shoulders a little lighter.

But as I rode in a cab on my way to the train station I had to ask the driver to stop, because the car seemed stifling. I got out and raced to the side of the bridge over the Schuylkill River, where I puked into the water. My stomach was still fluttering as I returned to the car, and I tried to settle myself down before arriving at the train station.

The Friday before the Women to Watch Luncheon, Ishmael and I made a quick jaunt to a bed and breakfast at Cape May, which was a soothing reprieve from the ridiculous pace I'd been keeping, but my nerves were still a bit frazzled. I tried to hide my anxiety from Ishmael, but the countless trips to the bathroom, where I vomited quietly behind the closed door, made him raise an eyebrow. It wasn't enough to deter him from showering me with kisses before explosive and steamy love sessions that lasted for hours.

When we pried our naked bodies away from each other late Saturday afternoon, we took a stroll through the shopping district, walking hand in hand as we peered into shop windows.

"Are you ready for everything that this new television show will bring?" he asked.

"What do you mean?"

"You know, the fame and the heightened attention that comes along with it."

"It's not like I'm Oprah or anything."

"Yet," he replied encouragingly. "But you know how those celebrities complain about reporters going through their trash cans and that they don't have any privacy."

"I've been dealing with that on a minor level for years. I don't see why this would be any different. Besides, I've always used the publicity to my advantage. Maybe I'll come up with a product to market so the fame will help with sales," I mused.

"Seriously, though. Folks will be looking into your past and interviewing people who met you, like, once. Are you ready for all of that?"

I paused for a second to contemplate the full impact. So far I had survived everything in my work unscathed, and truthfully I didn't see this show as being much different from what I'd been doing, so when I responded, "I've been scrutinized by worse," it was with confidence.

But a tinge of doubt lingered at the back of my mind.

Louise Harrison Simpson and The Coterie sent a limousine to pick me and Ishmael up at eleven o'clock on Sunday, March 1. There were peach and white roses in bunches on the backseat and a peach and white silk coat trimmed in Swarovski crystals in a box. A note inside the box said, "With our compliments, please wear this during the luncheon."

"It's beautiful," I remarked, wondering how much they had spent on the elegant jacket.

Shaking his head, Ishmael remarked, "These club women are something else. Dictating what you wear and stuff."

"It's okay with me. It's just an honor. This coat is like the PGA green jacket for golfers."

"Whatever," he said, laughing and rummaging through the large box of Godiva chocolates that was on the bar.

Jazz wafted through the rose-scented air as the car made its way along Lincoln Drive to Kelly Drive. Looking out the window at the runners sprinting along the Schuylkill River, I thought of how proud my mother would be of me.

I'd worked really hard, and this award, unlike the industry accolades that I received, was proof that I was doing good things in the community and that the folks recognized my growth and potential.

Ishmael snapped me out of my reverie, saying, "I know that there will be a lot of potential donors here."

"Ish, please don't work the room here."

"I won't. This is all about you today, baby. I'll just make initial contacts."

"That's fine."

The limo came to a stop in front of the hotel, and the chauffeur hopped out to open our doors. I slipped into the jacket before exiting and was greeted by a path of peach and white rose petals on the ground.

A smiling young woman in a peach-and-white suit met me in the lobby.

"Miss Harrison, what a pleasure it is to make your acquaintance. I'm Ruby Chambers."

"Miss Chambers, the pleasure is mine," I said in my confident on-air voice. "This is my friend Ishmael Taylor."

Ish nodded as the young woman smiled.

We were led into a banquet hall, where we were met with a standing ovation. Ruby led me to the raised dais, where Ishmael and I were seated next to the podium.

Louise approached me, smiling, with her arms open in preparation for an embrace.

"Welcome. I'm so glad that you could be here." She paused awkwardly before adding, "Sis."

My eyes filled immediately.

"No, no. Don't do that now. You'll mess up your makeup. We have a lifetime to catch up on. But now we're celebrating you."

A woman I assumed to be Evelyn Moore, Louise's co-chair, walked to the podium.

"Ladies and gentlemen, welcome to our twenty-fifth annual Women to Watch Luncheon. The Philadelphia Chapter of The Coterie is an organization of influential women committed to excellence and achievement. Every year the chapter gives $100,000 in scholarships to deserving young women who are poised to make their mark on society. Every year this chapter honors women who have already made an impression on society. Past honorees have included federal judges, college presidents, doctors, and entrepreneurs. This year we are honoring someone who hails from here and has made a big impact through her philanthropy and service. This year we are honoring Claudia 'Peach' Harrison."

The room broke into boisterous applause.

Evelyn read highlights of my biography before turning our attention to a large screen, with a picture of me as a child reciting the speech at St. Luke's church. My image was frozen, and I grinned broadly from the screen, my chubby cheeks making my face look like an apple. A collage of pictures flashed across the screen as background music filled the room. There were pictures of me in my school uniform, at the radio station, on Inner Circle trips, and there was one of me sitting with my father. I had no idea where that one had come from, and I dabbed at my eyes when it appeared on the screen. Ishmael held my hand under the table.

The photo montage sped forward to my early years as a reporter in the South. The changing hairstyles were enough to make me laugh aloud. Even with my voice silent on the large screen, I could tell by my demeanor how much my reporting style changed over time as I grew more comfortable on air.

After the montage ended, some familiar voices spoke from the screen. They were old coworkers who reminisced about my time at the various stations where I'd worked. There wasn't a lot that could be said, since I hadn't really socialized much with my coworkers, but they spoke about my talent and drive without making me sound like the bitch that I'd probably been. When the remembrances ended, Evelyn introduced a rising jazz singer with local roots who serenaded me with an original composition. After her performance, lunch was served.

I savored every bit of the salmon with peach glaze, risotto, and asparagus as the music from the live jazz band floated mellifluously through the hall. For dessert, a sampler of an individual peach cobbler, grilled peaches, and peach cheesecake with sliced peaches and crème fraîche was served.

More tributes were given after lunch, and again I found myself on the verge of tears as Louise got up and spoke about me. She spoke from the heart, telling of my determination, which she acknowledged even in my youth, and when she ended, she presented me with an award and a gift basket and she informed the crowd that I was being made an honorary member of The Coterie Inc., with all due rights and privileges. Then she hugged me, whispering, "It's your birthright."

Although I was being honored for my professional contributions, I was still choked up with emotion at the public recognition that I was getting. Ishmael saw my emotion, but he could never guess the depth from which it sprang. As we rode back to my apartment after the luncheon ended, he just held me as I cried tears of happiness.

23

June and July moved faster than a run in tissue silk, and I felt harried yet exhilarated as I conferred with network executives about contractual details. The new show was slated to air during Labor Day weekend, which was a major change in the ritualistic scheduling network. It appeared that one of their sure-to-be-a-hit-going-to-stay-on-the-air-for-years shows had completely tanked, so I was being brought in as a replacement of sorts. They were excited about it, and they promised heavy promotion to ensure success.

At work I was still enjoying myself, still researching ideas and pitching them to Diana, still interviewing local and celebrity guests, still making required appearances to promote the show, but all my duties were beginning to wear on me, and more of my workdays concluded with a nap. Ishmael would give me a wake-up call when he was leaving work, and a few nights a week we'd go out for dinner or he'd bring something over and we'd eat on the living room floor while watching a movie. While such a routine would be boring to some, it was a happy, familiar pattern that we looked forward to, kind of like the passive peace that I had been hoping for all of my life.

But my personal history should have warned me about getting lulled into complacency.

"Sweetness, are you still getting up early to work out?" he asked innocently.

Truthfully, I had intentions of working out every morning, but I'd been hitting the snooze button more frequently lately, which I admitted to him.

"Why don't you move your clock from your nightstand to your dresser?"

"So what are you saying?" I asked, stopping my hand midair, leaving my chicken cheese steak in limbo.

"Nothing, really. It just looks like you're getting a little puffy around the middle," he replied sheepishly, looking as if he didn't know whether to duck or brace himself.

"What?" I shrieked. He knew that, given my pudgy past, I was neurotic about my weight. I certainly couldn't pork up again now, especially with the new show pending.

"You're beautiful, baby, but you just look like you've been getting thicker. It looks good. In fact, in my neck of the woods they'd still call you skinny, but compared to normal, your breasts are bigger. I'm not complaining, though," he said, smiling. "Just observing."

I put my sandwich down and raced to the bathroom, where I dug out the scale from under some Epsom salts and rubbing alcohol in a corner of the closet. I usually gauged my weight according to the fit of my clothes, which had been a size four for years, so I rarely used the damn scale. Now Ishmael was telling me that I looked like I was about to go into hibernation, and that was the last thing that I needed.

Sure enough, the red number glaring angrily up at me was higher than I'd ever seen in adulthood, and I began to get nervous. I rushed out of the bathroom through the living room and into the kitchen, where I pulled open the refrigerator and freezer. It wasn't like the appliance had been filled with junk food, but I scanned the shelves looking for anything that seemed antithetical to healthy living.

"Are you going to eat the rest of this cheese steak?" Ishmael called from the living room.

My silence answered him as I pulled the trash can in front of the freezer, slam-dunking all my dairy products and anything that contained sugar. By the time I was finished, the only things that remained on the shelves were vegetables and lean meats. Then I headed for the cabinets, where I pulled every box of pasta, couscous, and rice from the shelves and introduced them to the dismissed dairy in the trash can.

Ishmael had planted himself at the doorway of the kitchen, where he watched me with amusement dancing in his eyes.

"There's nothing funny about this, Ish. My appearance is directly related to my work. I can't get fat."

"Have you thought that maybe it's not fat?"

"What are you talking about?" I asked with my head buried in another cabinet, where I spied an offending box of brownie mix that I kept around for when I had a sweet tooth.

"Why don't you make a doctor's appointment?"

"For what? I feel fine."

"If you say so."

I tried to fight my annoyance with him, blaming it on my hypersensitivity to this weight thing. He didn't understand. Although Philadelphia was a great city for news reporters of color, I didn't want to do anything that would potentially make my work more difficult. A male reporter could go bald and grow jowls like a Saint Bernard overnight, but a female reporter always had to be careful about her appearance. Discrimination of any kind was a downer, and I couldn't afford to make myself a mark.

"Okay, I'm going downstairs to work out. Feel free to join me, or just stay here," I said with an attitude, heading toward my bedroom to change into one of my designer sweatsuits.

"I think I'll head home. Claudia, don't sweat it, though. You look good, and five, ten, twenty pounds won't change that."

"Twenty pounds! Okay, now I know that you're crazy." I leaned up to kiss him before going into my closet. "See you."

"Bye, baby. Don't drive yourself crazy. You're going to be fine," he said, smiling and whistling as he walked down the hall toward the door.

I returned to my usual workout routine over the ensuing weeks, and I monitored my eating carefully, and I didn't gain any more, but I hadn't lost an ounce either. Maybe it was the stress of the transition I was in. Maybe age was finally creeping up on me. Whatever it was, I was so discouraged that I made a doctor's appointment, as Ishmael had initially suggested. He'd wanted to come with me, but I wouldn't let him. He relented only when I agreed to call him the moment I got home.

But I was too stunned with the news that the doctor delivered.

"You can't be serious," I said, looking Dr. Howard directly in her eyes.

"Of course, we don't have the official confirmation from your GYN yet, but all signs point to it."

"Pregnant?"

"Yes. You can't remember your last period . . ."

"I've always been irregular. Sometimes I might go two months without a period," I interrupted, as if fighting her would change my results.

"You're exhausted . . ."

"I work a lot."

"Your breasts are tender."

I didn't have a rebuttal for that, so I just sank into the chair, trying to hold back the tears.

She patted my hand, saying, "It's really a blessing. Think of how many people want babies and can't have them."

Her words went right over my head. "It couldn't come at a worse time," I whined, thinking about the show. Then a bigger issue popped into my head: "If I'm ten weeks pregnant, like she thinks I am, the baby could belong to one of two people." That reality smacked me in the face, and I began wailing in her office. I hadn't been worried about catching an STD from Ishmael or from Thomas, so I'd taken the pill with regularity. But then I'd had that yeast infection, and I'd had to take an antibiotic, which, of course, lessened the effectiveness of the pill.

Dr. Howard looked confused, then sympathetic, as she reached out to pat my hand. "Is there someone you'd like me to call?"

There was no one I wanted to see at that moment, so I shook my head no and reached in my purse for my keys. I grabbed the box of tissues from her desk and hurried out of her office, hearing her call behind me, "Make an appointment with your gynecologist as soon as possible. You need to begin prenatal care if you're going to continue with this pregnancy."

My head swirled as I drove home. How could I have let this happen? I hadn't gone down and back up the East Coast to wind up just like my mother, a woman never to fulfill her full potential, bringing another bastard into the world. Unmarried. I refused to do it. To have all those highbrow folks on both sides of the color line look at me like I was a statistic, another hot-to-trot black woman fouling up the next generation by being stupid enough to get knocked up and not get a ring. Absolutely not. No child of mine was going to perpetuate the stereotypical cycle. I'd never have that on my conscience. Besides, I had so much terrain left to explore, and I refused to be saddled with such a responsibility on my own.

I thought of my options. Thomas Brooks was too kind a man to be dragged through the mud by allegations of having had a child out of wedlock. That wouldn't look any better than my having the child alone. Never mind the fact that he was my brother-in-law. I'd be painted as a cheap harlot despite the fact that his home was already wrecked before I showed up on the scene.

That left me with one option, and when I thought about it, it wasn't a bad one. While we'd rely on my salary for the lifestyle that I desired, Ishmael was a wonderful man, and he would make a wonderful father. The more I drummed that into my head, the better I felt, so by the time I got home, my tears had subsided, and I thought about how to tell him the news.

I didn't have long to prepare, because he was waiting in the lobby of my building when I arrived.

I approached him slowly, noting the worry etched on his face. He hugged and kissed me, saying, "Hey, sweetness. How do you feel?"

I nodded, saying nothing while a vestigial shudder passed over me.

"What did the doctor say?"

Searching his face, I saw concern, love, and respect, and I knew that I was making the right choice when I said, "You're going to be a father."

A howl broke forth from his gut, and he shook his fist in victory, saying, "I knew it. Whew, baby! That's great news."

I didn't imagine that he'd be so happy, and the shock must have registered on my face, because when he came down from his high, he asked, "What's wrong?"

"I'm not married," I blurted out.

Ishmael wrapped his arms around me, thoroughly enveloping me as he kissed my forehead.

"Don't worry," he reassured me.

"How can you say that? Maybe it doesn't mean anything to you, but I want my child to have a name. I want her to have two parents who live in the same home. I want her to . . . to . . . not be a . . ."

I refused to say the word aloud, and I lowered my head, wondering what he would do. Would he step up and do the honorable thing? Would he leave me hanging? Would he make sure that we were taken care of the way a man should? The anxiety racing through me forced tears to return, and I leaned against him and cried.

"Aw, baby, don't cry," he said softly, trying to shush me. "Claudia, don't cry."

When my tears continued, he gently wrapped an arm around me, leading me through the lobby doors and outside to his car. "Let's take a ride," he suggested, helping me into the car.

I silently complied with his request and stretched the seatbelt over my little passenger. Ishmael came around to the driver's side and got in, still smiling. He turned on Temple University's jazz station, and we drove wordlessly along Kelly Drive toward Center City. When we got to the art museum area, he parked the car, then he hopped out, coming around to the other side to help me out. He wrapped his hand around mine, and we started walking toward the art museum steps. Tourists were still doing their best Rocky Balboa impersonations as we slowly mounted the marble slabs where we had ended up the first night after our tour of Camden. When we got to the top, he sat down and pulled me onto his lap. Kissing my cheeks, he smiled again.

"Claudia, you have nothing to worry about. I'm here, and I'm always going to be here. You know how much I suffered, growing up without a man in my home, and I'd never wish that on any child, especially on a child of mine. When I was growing up, I used to hate to hear people criticizing their fathers, talking about how much their dads got on their nerves. They never understood that I would have taken the pitiful fathers that they were trashing any day over the empty space in my house where he was supposed to be. My foster father filled a lot of that void, but I knew that no matter how much he treated me like a son, he still wasn't my official father. And I know that you missed out on having your dad in your life like you wanted, and you probably promised never to let your child endure the same thing.

"Well, Claudia, I knew before you did that you were pregnant. I was just waiting for confirmation from your doctor. Even if that hadn't come up, I still knew the first time we sat here that I wanted you in my life for the duration. And you don't deserve anything less than all of me."

He fumbled in his pocket, pulling out a small white box.

"I can't get any lower than this since you're sitting on my lap, but just imagine that I'm on my knee as I ask you if you'll do me the honor of becoming Mrs. Ishmael Taylor."

My breath caught in my throat as I looked at the beautiful ring. For the third time that evening, my eyes filled with tears, and I was rendered speechless.

"You've got to say something, baby, so I know what you're thinking."

"Yes. Yes. Yes. Ishmael Taylor, I'll marry you!" I screamed, standing up. He joined me in standing on the top step, and as we stood with the city below us, Ishmael Taylor kissed me, and I felt every fear, every moment of anxiety, every ounce of tension melt, leaving my head, coursing down my throat, pulsing through my chest, and swirling down into my stomach, which trembled in response.

24

I thought that it was incredibly tacky to get married with a protruding belly, so the following weeks were a flurry of activity as Ishmael and I planned our nuptials for the weekend before Labor Day weekend. I had to scurry and plead a bit to get the accommodations that I wanted, but everything was taking shape as planned. I hired someone to hand-deliver the engraved invitations in July to give it a personal touch.

Miss Mamie came up to help me, and as she carried out my wishes, commanding business owners to comply with my requests, I actually felt like a bit of a princess. Ishmael left the details to us, and he checked in a few times a day to make sure that I was feeling okay and to see if there was anything that I needed him to do. We made kissy noises as Miss Mamie hurried us off the phone, reminding me that we had a ton of work to do.

Regretfully, I stopped working, and I was pretty sad about that, because I really loved my job. I knew that I needed to rest up, though, before beginning the promotional rounds for the new job. I'd spoken with the producers, telling them about the pregnancy, and we agreed that I'd tape as many as three shows a day for a few weeks to make up for the six weeks of maternity leave that I would take. It was a grueling schedule, but I was fine with it, having already learned that sacrifice is necessary for the completion of a goal.

Miss Mamie had gone with me to New York to meet with the producers, and we had decided to make a day of it with shopping, lunch, and people watching added in for good measure, and I was growing more and more optimistic about the way my life was taking shape.

But optimism and hope are two sisters that wanted nothing to do with me.

It had started simply. The producer said, "You know, to give the audience a better picture of who Peach Harrison is, why don't we interview some family members, like your aunt Mamie, and we can use snippets from the conversation in the promos that we're running."

"Won't they get to know who I am simply by watching the show?" I asked. The last thing that I wanted was to have my past dredged up, embarrassing me, drawling about how I was always a sweet little stuttering, fat girl who helped Momma complete her chores at the Harrisons' home before we returned to our rented house.

"They will, but this will draw them in. Show them your down-to-earth, human side."

"They'll see that soon enough."

"We need to hook them, Peach. You're beautiful, and our country is obsessed with beauty, but we need to establish longevity for you, and the best way to do that is to show that you're more than just a pretty face. You've got talent, good morals, and common sense."

"I thank you for your compliments, but I'd like to pass on that idea," I said, hoping to put the issue to bed.

"Okay. We'll think of a different angle, and we'll run it past you."

A few days later, he called back. "How about if we go to your old neighborhood and interview some people you grew up with, and folks who remember you? Neighbors and such."

That thought made me cringe even more. Although I couldn't play the privileged-childhood card on my old turf in Philadelphia, I certainly didn't want people across the country to know that, before I was run out of town, my neighborhood, which hadn't seemed so terrible when I was living there, was now another enclave ravaged by crack.

"No, thank you," I told him politely, trying to avoid earning the reputation of being a diva who was difficult to work with.

The producer didn't call back for a while, and the next time he did, he didn't make suggestions. He simply said that pre-production was beginning, and that he'd be in contact soon.

Again I immersed myself in the wedding plans and tried to fight off the fatigue that plagued me by the end of the day. I was into my second trimester, and I was feeling better than I had in the first, but I was starting to show, and I wasn't ready to have it known that I was pregnant without the benefit of marriage yet. Late August couldn't come soon enough.

But then the first shoe fell.

"Hello," I slurred, answering the phone by my bed one morning. Without pushing my eye mask out of the way, I knew that the sky was still relatively dark, and phone calls in the dark could only mean trouble.

"Peach, it appears that we have a bit of a problem," the voice said.

"I'm sorry. Who is this?"

"Peter Mercer, the executive producer of *Life's a Peach*. We're not going to move ahead with the show."

"Why? Did I do something wrong?" I asked frantically.

"No. It was an executive decision, and we've simply decided to try something different."

"But wait. I can be different. If you want edgy, I can give you edgy. If you want sweet, I can do that, too. I'm flexible."

"Peach, I assure you that it has nothing to do with you. Things like this happen all the time. It's nothing personal. We'll still send you a check for half the amount that you were supposed to get for the season. Really, there are no hard feelings. Maybe it's something that we can revisit at a later date."

"But I've already quit my job at the station."

"You're talented. You'll find work again in another market. I can send you some leads. Besides, the check will more than cover you for a while."

"And there's nothing that I can do?" I asked quietly. At this point I was desperate enough to sleep with him sight unseen to save my show.

"No. Just keep doing good work. I'm almost certain that your name will come up again."

"Thanks for your confidence. Have a good day."

"Best wishes, Peach."

I threw the phone at the wall and screamed in horror. Moments later I heard Miss Mamie outside my door, clambering to get in.

"Claudia!" she shouted. "Claudia, are you okay?"

"Go away!"

"Open the door, baby," she coaxed.

"I said go away!" I screamed again.

"Just let me know you're okay."

"No, I'm not. Just leave me alone. I'm not hurt, but please leave me alone."

She pleaded with me for what seemed like hours before I finally opened the door, and then it was only after she threatened to call Ishmael. I didn't want to tell him that I was a failure, so I relented and let her in.

"What's the matter?"

"There isn't going to be a show."

"Aw, baby, why not?"

"They've decided to do something different. It's as simple as that."

"Do you want me to talk to them? I can help straighten things out, let them know that you're such a good girl. And you always—"

"There's nothing to straighten out, Miss Mamie. What's done is done. It's over," I said, flopping on the bed.

"Be careful, child," Miss Mamie cautioned. "You don't want to hurt that baby."

I turned to look at her, and put my hand on my stomach protectively. I had someone else to consider now, and that knowledge scared me more than ever. I sighed, turning over onto my side and balling up in a fetal position as the tears poured out of my eyes.

Miss Mamie didn't know what to tell Ishmael when he came over that evening, so she said nothing, continuing with the wedding plans like business as usual. But Ishmael knew that something was wrong.

He sat on the edge of my bed as I told him that the show had been canceled. He held me close, not asking for an explanation, just trying to comfort me. And that made me feel even worse. Here he was, supporting me, and he didn't even know that I was deceiving him. He was about to marry me, never guessing that the child I was carrying might not be his. Did I deserve such a man? He never looked beyond my words for deeper meanings and potential lies. He just accepted what I told him. I pulled him close to me and cried, and he never imagined that my tears ran deeper than he could ever know.

Days crept by as I stayed holed up in my apartment. Philadelphia with all of its lies about brotherly love and sisterly affection was the last place that I wanted to be right then. I wanted to be on my honeymoon in Aruba.

But I soon found out that that wouldn't happen either.

While Miss Mamie was immersed in the last-minute details of the wedding plans, Ishmael and I used the time to reconnect with each other. It had been awhile since we had made love, and as we were reintroduced to each other's bodies, I felt a sense of contentment that almost made up for the disappointment of losing the show. Morning light crept upon us one day in mid-August, and as I lay next to him, watching his chest rise and fall with gentle snores, I smiled, reminded of how much I loved this man.

He sensed me looking at him, and he woke up smiling. "What are you thinking about?" he asked groggily.

"I'm thinking about how good a man you are," I admitted.

"And don't you forget it," he teased.

"I won't."

And I didn't forget it, even after what came later in the day.

Miss Mamie answered the door, and Elizabeth Harrison Brooks stepped in without waiting to be invited.

"I'm here to see Claudia," she said, without giving Miss Mamie a respectful, proper greeting.

Folding her arms across her chest, Miss Mamie asked, "About what?"

"Just get her out here, or I'll find her myself," Elizabeth commanded loudly.

I heard her voice from the kitchen, where Ishmael and I were going over the seating arrangements for the wedding. Recognizing her voice, I stood, looked at Ishmael, and kissed him on the lips, saying, "I love you."

Worry passed over his face as he heard the loud voice, and he followed me as I walked into the living room to face Elizabeth.

"I don't know how you did it or why, but you did," she sneered at me. "And you bought him cheaply. With jewelry."

She threw the pair of platinum cuff links onto the coffee table, and their clatter seemed deafening.

248

"Wait a second here," Ishmael said, stepping toward her, ready to herd her out the door. "You can't come in here throwing this around. This isn't—"

"Ishmael, it's okay," I said, putting a hand on his arm and stepping forward.

"My husband. You had to sleep with my husband! Are you happy with yourself? Did it make you feel like a big woman to bed him? Why did you do it? To spite me?"

I stared at her with a smirk on my face and my chin held high, but the satisfaction that I had felt began to dissipate when Ishmael picked up the cuff links from the table. His shoulders slumped, and he turned his head to look at me.

"Does he know what a tramp you are? Or do you have him fooled into thinking that you're a sweet angel? Huh? Answer me!" she shouted.

Miss Mamie stepped in. "Look here, honey. You're going to turn around and—"

Elizabeth interrupted her, turning back to me. "So now you've got nothing to say, huh? I bet that you had a lot of pillow talk for my husband."

She turned her attention to Ishmael. "You put a ring on her finger? Are you crazy? She's a worthless whore. Just like her mother."

She turned her attention to me again. "I ought to slap you back to Georgia, you tramp," she sneered before spitting on my carpet. "You're finished here. Don't you ever show your face around here again. Do you hear me? Don't ever show your face around here again!"

With that, Elizabeth turned on her heel and stormed out as quickly as she'd arrived, and the whirlwind that I'd created and that she'd dredged up was irreparable.

"Ishmael," I said, not daring to cry but feeling all of his pain in my own chest. I reached out to touch his arm.

"Don't touch me, Claudia," he said, snatching his arm out of my grasp.

"No, Ish, please listen to me. I can explain. It was all a mistake. I didn't mean to—"

"Claudia, is it true?" he said, trying to look me in the eye through the tears that were brimming in his own.

My silence was all the answer that he needed.

"Some mistakes don't deserve second chances," he said. Then he walked down the hall to my bedroom to gather his things.

As he tried to leave I dove toward his legs, trying to make him stay.

"Get up, Claudia," he said coldly. "You might hurt yourself and the baby, whoever's it is."

The brunt of his words made me let go of his leg, and I watched his feet as they walked out the door.

I lay crumpled in a heap for hours, calling his name and wailing as if my heart had been ripped from my body.

I tried to reposition myself to rise again from the ashes like a phoenix, calling my general manager from the station and attempting to get my job back, but scandal flies fast in the city, and they wanted no part of me. Miss Mamie wanted me to come back to Georgia, but there was no way I could go back there. I refused to spend the rest of my days rotting on her front porch while life passed me by, but I didn't tell her that. I sent her ahead of me, telling her that I was tying up some loose ends in the city and waiting for my FBC check to arrive. But mostly I was plotting my arrival in a new place. I was angry and bitter, but I had no one to blame but myself. Right or wrong, I had made my own decisions, and now I had to live with the consequences. But as I looked around the apartment one last time, I knew that I, Peach Harrison, would rise again.

Readers' Guide

1. While Claudia bears emotional scars from her youth, were there any benefits to growing up so closely to the moneyed Harrison clan?

2. Why is young Claudia so reluctant to tell anyone about the abuse she suffers from Eliza Harrison?

3. Eliza and her daughters clearly come across as malevolent characters. Does Louis Harrison share in any of the blame?

4. Revenge ultimately leads to Peach's undoing. Why can't she simply put the past where it belongs?

5. Many of the female characters, like Miss Mamie, Eliza, Elizabeth, Louise, Elicia, and Lindsay, learn at young ages

that their beauty is a valuable commodity. Is this a lesson that we really want to pass on to our daughters, or does society force our hands?

6. Why does Thomas Brooks continue his affair with Peach even after he learns of her identity?

7. Does Ishmael really know Peach? If so, what does he see as her redeeming qualities? If not, whose fault is it that he doesn't know her?

8. Dr. and Mrs. John Freeman, along with Louis and Eliza Harrison, demonstrate that there are trade-offs in every relationship. Are their sacrifices more than you'd be willing to handle?

9. Revenge is something that many of us contemplate and some of us even act upon. Have you ever done anything for the sake of revenge that you now regret?

10. Class is an important backdrop in this story, and skin color (not race) is linked with class, as evidenced by Eliza's father and even Louis Harrison. In your own experiences and observations, have you seen evidence of the schism that can occur between those of varying skin color?

About the Author

Nicole Bailey-Williams, the author of *A Little Piece of Sky* and *Floating*, is a high school English teacher and former host of *The Literary Review*, a Philadelphia radio show that ran for nine years. Her writing has appeared in a variety of publications, including *Publishers Weekly*, *Black Issues Book Review*, and *Gumbo: An Anthology of African American Writing*. She lives in New Jersey.